Kindred spirit . . . or immortal enemy?

I collected my books and approached the teacher's desk just as the last kid banged out the door. Ms. Larch's glinting green eyes followed me with amusement. I wondered if this was what a mouse saw when it came upon a cat.

"Ms. Larch?"

She steepled her slender fingers beneath her chin. "Yes, Svetlana?" Her red mouth curled at the corners.

I concentrated, forming the words in my mind. *Can you hear me?* I thought, directing my words into her head.

Her eyes went wide in slight amusement. "Of course I can hear you," she replied.

I knew it was real, but there was still a part of me that didn't believe it could be happening. I stood frozen before her desk.

She laughed.

Had I thought that I'd only imagined her words in my mind yesterday? Was this really possible? *Are you . . . like me?* I spilled the question without thinking, and suddenly found myself quivering in anticipation, hanging on the answer.

"Like you?" The expression over her face turned quizzical. She reached and tapped a red fingernail to her lips. Her green eyes sparkled, amused. "And what . . . are you like, Svetlana?"

"A . . . vampire?" I whispered.

Bar Code →

sandpiper

HOUGHTON MIFFLIN HARCOURT

BOSTON • NEW YORK

Many thanks to my awesome agent, Erin Murphy, my excellent
editor, Jennifer Wingertzhan, and all the folks at Clarion Books who have
made Svetlana Grimm come to life. And to Lisa Gordon, without whose
support and encouragement none of it would be possible.

Published in the United States by Sandpiper, an imprint of Houghton
Mifflin Harcourt Publishing Company. Originally published in hardcover
in the United States by Clarion Books, an imprint of Houghton Mifflin
Harcourt Publishing Company, 2009.

SANDPIPER and the SANDPIPER logo are trademarks of Houghton
Mifflin Harcourt Publishing Company.

For information about permission to reproduce
selections from this book, write to Permissions,
Houghton Mifflin Harcourt Publishing Company,
215 Park Avenue South, New York, New York 10003.

www.hmhbooks.com

The text of this book is set in 12-point Bembo.

The Library of Congress has cataloged the hardcover edition as follows:
Harris, Lewis, 1964–
A taste for red / by Lewis Harris.
p. cm.
Summary: When some of her classmates disappear, sixth-grader Svetlana,
along with her new friends, goes in search of the missing students using her
newfound ability as an Olfactive, one who has heightened smell, hearing,
and the ability to detect vampires.

ISBN: 978-0-547-14462-7 hardcover
ISBN: 978-0-547-39851-8 paperback
[1. Vampires—Fiction. 2. Missing children—Fiction. 3. Friendship—Fiction.] I. Title
PZ7.H24217Tas 2009   [Fic]—dc22   2008025318

Manufactured in the United States of America
DOM 10 9 8 7 6 5 4 3 2 1

For Albert Lewis Harris Sr. and Mary Ann Carrico

One

$\mathcal{B}$eing a vampire is a solitary business—or had been, until now. For months I lived in seclusion behind the walls of Grimm Manor. I secretly watched the world from the shadows of Morgloom Woods. I spied on unsuspecting neighbors, studied the comings and goings of innocent children at play up and down the tree-lined sidewalks of Cherry Street. Unseen and protected within the walls of my hidden lair high atop the Oak of Doom, I saw it all. I knew every inch of the family grounds, every twisted tree and blade of grass. I knew where my dog, Razor, had buried every bone. Unfortunately, I was unable to remain hidden forever. I was compelled to leave my secret world and venture into the unknown. On orders from my parents, and against my deepest wishes, I was forced to attend sixth grade at Sunny Hill Middle School.

Thwack! Thwack! Thwack!

Mr. Dumloch, horrible and fat, stood at the front of the classroom and whacked his ruler against the top of his desk. It was my first morning. The mob of kids ceased shouting, brought their annoying laughter to an abrupt halt, and turned a roomful of curious eyes to stare. How ridiculous they looked. I stood alongside the cologne-soaked teacher and tried my best not to breathe. What did he do, bathe in the stuff?

"All right, everyone, be quiet," Dumloch began, grumbling, his drooping jowls quivering like Jell-O. His cheap scent made me dizzy. "We have a new student joining us today. This is Stephanie—"

"Svetlana," I corrected, cringing. I despised the name Stephanie! How could my parents have been so cruel?

"What's that?" Dumloch peered down at me through round spectacles; his wiry eyebrows clutched like kissing caterpillars.

"Sss-vet-LAH-nah," I repeated, looking up at the poor man's silly face. "It's Romanian."

"Oh, you're Romanian?" he asked, feigning interest. He pasted a cardboard smile across his chubby face. His teeth were stained an awful yellow and in desperate need of a cleaning ASAP—as soon as possible.

Call the dentist, Dumloch, I thought, smiling my own false smile as I sent him the thought. I said, "I'm from Texas, actually." His smile waned. Could this sad specimen of an instructor possibly teach me anything? I doubted it; I was certain the man didn't even floss.

"Well, anyway." He cleared his throat. "Let's everybody welcome . . . Svetlana Grimm."

"Welcome, Svetlana!" the kids sang in unison.

Ugh. It was the opposite of music to my ears.

I followed Dumloch's pointing finger to the only empty seat in the classroom—as if I couldn't have figured that one out for myself. I passed through the whispers and stares and slid my stack of newly issued textbooks beneath the desk, all but world history, which I needed for this, the first class of what was certain to be a very, very long day.

The girl seated at the desk in front of me turned and told me her name was Sandy Cross. "I've seen you," she said. "You live on Cherry Street next to the Bone Lady."

What! How did this mischievous minx know me? The Bone Lady? She must have meant Lenora Bones, the skeletal old woman who had recently moved into the brick house next door. I'd read the name on the mailbox in front of the house during one of my clandestine explorations of the neighborhood. I wrinkled my nose at the annoying girl's bubblegum breath. Did she chew gum for breakfast? And what was with her crazy hair? It looked as if someone had replaced her real hair with a wig of blond yarn and then jammed her fingers into an electrical outlet. I could hardly see beyond the mass of frizz to Dumpy Dumloch sitting before the classroom, following his finger as he read down the roll.

Sandy Cross went on, "You live in the house with the mean dog and your dad drives a green car, am I right? The big house with the tall fence, right? My dad hates that fence. He wants to know why your dad painted it black."

Who was this girl? Had she been spying on me? And

what did she mean by "mean dog"? My lovable Razor was a perfect dog, a pure angel—unless you messed with me, of course, and then you were dog food. "How do you know all this?" I asked, trying not to reveal my displeasure.

"I live in the corner house—the one with the trampoline. I'm sure you've seen it."

Of course! One of the trampoline kids! Now I recognized that big bush of yellow hair. I'd seen Little Miss Bubblegum plenty of times, bouncing like a lunatic in her front yard.

"Why don't you ever come outside?" Sandy Cross asked. She threw a thumb to her left and said, "This is Dwight Foote. He lives two streets over on Mango Court."

The kid next to her, I'm not kidding, had a head as big as a basketball. He wore moonpie-thick glasses that magnified his eyeballs into giant blinking blueberries.

"Yeah, I've seen you, too," he chimed in. "You're always up in that tree house."

The Oak of Doom! Did everyone in this crummy school know my business?

"You're the girl with the binoculars."

This last remark came from the boy seated behind me, an Asian kid with a mouthful of braces.

I was surrounded by hostiles!

"I'm a bird watcher," I explained.

"Yeah? Me, too," Dwight Foote said excitedly, his blueberry eyes widening. "Me and my dad keep an alphabetical and numerical record of all the types of birds that visit the feeders in our yard. Do you have any bird feeders? We have two in the front yard and one in the back. We mostly get bluejays in the—"

"Can it, Foote," Sandy ordered. "This girl isn't a bird watcher, she's a spy."

A spy! What a vile accusation! True, but extremely rude. I could, however, easily handle the situation. I said, "It's a scientific fact that bird feeders upset a bird's natural ability to fend for itself in the wild. I choose to enjoy birds in an undisturbed habitat, especially the playful games of the red-breasted robin. I also appreciate the majestic cardinal, whose—"

"Uh-huh," Sandy interrupted. "Sure you do . . . spy."

"Why haven't you come to school before now?" the Asian kid asked. He raised his hand and answered "Here" after Dumloch called the name Fumio Chen.

"I'm home-schooled," I answered. "Or I *was* home-schooled. My mom started a new job today." As a substitute teacher—of all things! Now she'd be teaching mobs of strange kids just like Dumpy Dumloch did. How could that be more rewarding than teaching brilliant me?

"You'll like it here," Fumio predicted.

"Sunny Hill is an awesome school," Foote promised.

But despite assurances, the day began poorly. Not only did Dumloch smell like a puddle of cheap perfume, he was also a terrible teacher. History class was *boring*. My mom could teach circles around Mr. Dumloch. All he did was read from the book—*blah, blah, blah*. Very lame. He didn't incorporate any funny voices or act out any stories or make any portion of the class the least bit interesting. How was I going to remain awake in his classroom day after day? It was total torture. After history came math—predictably awful, definitely not the subject where my fancy takes flight. I think the teacher had a glass eye, though, so that was somewhat cool. Then gym class, which was gross—I'm never happy in shorts.

Never.

After that, it was time to head to the cafeteria for lunch. Since I eat only red foods, I'd brought my lunch along with me. In vampire movies, Hollywood hacks perpetuate the myth that a vampire must drink blood in order to survive, which is simply not true. Think about it: How can anyone live by drinking blood? That might work for a mosquito, but it's not fit food for an advanced specimen lording over the top of the food chain, is it? I'm a vampire, not a tick. The truth is, real vampires can eat any food—so long as it's red. For lunch I had packed a box of cranberry juice, sliced strawberries, a ham sandwich (white foods are neutral, so removing the crust from white bread makes it perfectly edible), and a wedge of red velvet cake.

As I feasted, Dwight Foote plopped down on the bench across the table from me. He had a plate full of spaghetti—which would've been fine for me to eat if I'd picked the green peppers from the sauce.

"What classes do you have after lunch, Svetlana?" he asked, cramming a mouthful of pasta into his big head, sucking up a wayward strand of noodle, and throwing tomato sauce onto his thick eyeglasses. He swiped the cuff of his shirtsleeve across the lens.

Charming.

"English and then science," I said.

"Cool. I've got Ms. Larch for last-period science, too. She just started teaching here after Mr. Boyd went on the lam."

"On the lam?" What was this kid talking about?

"Blew town," he said. "Vanished. Mr. Boyd's class was a cakewalk, but Ms. Larch is a royal pain." He shook his big head, frowning. "Her science class is hard—I'm talking *Jeopardy* hard." His giant eyes swam like blue fish behind his glasses. *Blink. Blink.* "But after lunch, I go to gym—which I'm excellent at. I might be the fastest guy in the whole school. Right now my ankles are pretty swollen, though. Too many squat thrusts, I think. Soon as they heal up, I'll probably go out for track or football or basketball or wrestling or golf." A meatball dropped off his fork and fell into his lap.

Oh, brother. Who was this guy kidding? I tried to probe his mind, but there was nothing there. A vampire has extrasensory perception—ESP, you know? I can sometimes read a person's thoughts or even control the physical body if the victim's brain is sufficiently developed. Apparently, Foote's lame brain was too small for my vampire powers to find purchase.

From the other side of the cafeteria, the poofy-haired blond, Sandy Cross, approached with two giggling friends in tow. "How's your first day of school going, Stephanie?" she asked sweetly. Her lips curled into a sugary smile that I wanted to wipe off her dimpled face.

Stephanie! How dare she call me by that horrid name! If I *were* a bloodsucker, she'd be the first one drained. But

I wouldn't give her the satisfaction of seeing me ruffled. I wouldn't allow myself to be irritated by her intentional use of that oh-so-boring name. I smiled, thinking that Stephanie was nearly as bland as the name "Sandy"—if that was possible.

"The name is Svetlana," I corrected.

"Oh, that's right." She was all dimples, teeth, and hair. She wore a hideous pink belt and a too tacky seashell necklace. She had rhinestones fastened to the pockets of her jeans.

I'm not kidding.

Her two friends were obviously sisters and equally fashion challenged—cloned Barbie doll–types wearing identical pink belts and the same dopey seashell necklaces. One was as thin as the spaghetti disappearing off Foote's plate, and the other was even skinnier than that. They clung to either side of Sandy Cross like parentheses.

"This is Marsha and Madison," Sandy said.

Of course they were.

The thinner one, Madison, said, "You shouldn't wear all black. It makes your skin look washed out." Fashion criticism from one-half of the number 11—perfect. I looked down at my favorite black T-shirt, black pants, and black shoes. My fingernails were painted midnight black to match my raven hair.

"You look kind of like a mime," squeaked the other one, Marsha.

"My dad thinks mimes are stupid," Sandy added. Her rosy chipmunk cheeks glowed.

What *would* blood taste like, I wondered?

During lunch I had decided that Sandy Cross and her cronies would become my archenemies, but I was wrong—that distinction went to Ms. Sylvia Larch, my science teacher.

"Svetlana, please come to the front of the classroom and introduce yourself. Tell us a little bit about who you are." Ms. Larch stabbed a glossy red fingernail at a spot alongside her desk where she wished me to stand and display myself for her and the class's amusement.

How cruel she was—yet beautiful. Her hair was as straight and as black as my own. Her skin, like mine, was as pale as ivory. She was considerably taller than I was, and she stood poised before the chalkboard on spiked high heels that were blood-red and as sharp as daggers. She didn't smell too swell, though. There was a whiff of something slightly rotted about her—a little like a pound of hamburger that has remained outside the refrigerator too long.

"Don't be shy," she suggested, wiggling me forward with a wormy finger, enjoying my discomfort.

I loathed having to speak in front of the class! Who wouldn't? What an abuse of power! Heartless woman. I locked my hands together across my waist and stood before the staring mob of mouth-breathers. To my embarrassment, my hands trembled. What did I have to be nervous about? What did I have to fear from these ... these ...

"My name is Svetlana—"

"*Louder,* please." Ms. Larch demonstrated, raising her voice while dropping her svelte figure into the chair behind her desk and swiveling around to observe me squirming before the class.

I stared daggers into her green eyes, boring into her mind with my vampiric control. I willed her to instruct me to return to my seat. I took control of her brain and moved her lips to speak the words I wished to hear.

"Tell us where you're from, Svetlana," she said instead, brushing aside my psychic efforts.

She was powerful.

I turned my gaze back to the roomful of pitiful faces and decided to just get it over with. "I'm Svetlana Grimm, and ... I ... um, moved here from, uh, Texas." I stammered, searching for words. "I have a dog named Razor. . . ." What could I say? What did these jellybean-eaters need to know?

Ms. Larch asked, "Your file says you've always been home-schooled. Is that correct, Svetlana?" Her wire-thin eyebrows were drawn back like tiny mousetraps. "Having the opportunity to engage your peers must be an exciting experience for you."

So she had a secret file on me. And as far as engaging my peers went, it was about on par with being poked over and over again in the eye. "It's okay," I lied.

"Well, I hope it will end up being better than *okay*," she purred, her lips turning upward into a sly smile while her green eyes remained hard as stones.

I returned to my desk as Ms. Larch moved to the corner of the classroom, where she uncovered a television screen. She inserted an instructional film and asked Fumio Chen to pull down the shades. As Fumio eagerly complied, the science teacher began the movie, then turned off the lights and left the room. A few kids whispered and passed notes back and forth while the lesson played, but most watched, glued to the program. The film demonstrated an experiment in which a rodent was trained to navigate a maze by being subjected to an electrical shock whenever it chose the wrong course. The rat eventually succeeded in making its way through the maze, but its rodent expression remained unreadable; it was impossible to say how the rat felt about its sad situation. There was cheese at the end, so I guess that was something; but I couldn't help feeling sorry for the poor creature.

"No pain, no gain," Ms. Larch pronounced as she re-entered the room, snapping on the overhead lights and dazzling our eyes. She set aside a covered plate she'd brought back with her, stopping the film as it finished. "Can anyone relate to the rat?" she asked with a grin, pulling perfect supermodel lips back over a row of sparkling teeth. "Believe me, that was a life lesson, not just science." She prattled on about negative reinforcement and Pavlovian conditioning and other such scientific gobbledy-gook. Eventually, the bell rang for the end of school, and everyone jumped from their seats, grabbing and shuffling for bags and books.

"As you leave, please feel free to pop a treat into your mouth!" Ms. Larch uncovered the plate she'd brought back, revealing a mound of chocolate squares. The room erupted with inspired cries of what a wonderful teacher she was and how exciting and fun science could be. What a bunch of suck-ups! As the students passed, they all reached eagerly for the plate, plucking a chocolate.

"Pop it right into your mouth—we don't want a mess," Larch instructed, waving the rabble of kids along.

I passed without taking a treat, and Ms. Larch dropped a surprisingly strong hand onto my shoulder, pulling me aside. "Just one moment, please, Svetlana."

Dwight Foote reached around me and grabbed a square of chocolate, gulping it down and reaching for a second.

"Help yourself to another chocolate, Dwight," Ms. Larch encouraged. "I don't think Svetlana wants her piece."

"My dad's picking me—" I started.

"You can wait a moment," the science teacher interrupted, silencing me with a flash of electric-green eyes.

Fumio Chen was the last student to leave. "Ms. Larch, can I ask you—"

"Tomorrow, Fumio," Larch insisted, setting the remaining chocolates aside. She propelled him out the door with a shove, pulling the door closed with a click. "Svetlana." She whirled, crossing her arms and drumming her red nails over her pale skin. "Have a chocolate." She picked up the plate, pushing it toward me.

The sweet cocoa smell mixed with her meaty odor turned my stomach. I stepped away, fighting the urge to gag. "No, thank you! My dad's waiting."

"Well, of course he is—it being your first day at school. I've only recently moved to Sunny Hill myself." She lowered the plate of chocolates and reached into her jacket pocket. "It's so nice to have another new face around. I sense something very special about you, Svetlana. Do you feel it? You don't seem at all excited by the chocolates, though."

A tingling of alarm tickled the tiny hairs on my arms and neck. Ms. Larch stepped closer. Her overripe, rotting odor filled my nose. I backed away until the chalkboard pressed at my back. Panic coursed the length of me, rippling from head to toe. I met her glassy green stare, and the panic subsided. Her eyes narrowed like a cat's into twin slivers of green moon.

Sweet Svetlana, I know who you are. The teacher's silken words whispered inside my mind, but her lips never moved! Her thoughts uncoiled behind my eyes like an invading serpent. She was inside my head! *I bet you'd rather have an apple, wouldn't you? One that's nice and . . . red.*

I tore my stare from her laughing eyes, dropping my gaze to the glistening red apple she'd drawn from her jacket pocket. Raw fear splashed through my insides like water from a ruptured balloon. I rushed for the door, flinging it open with a bang. I bolted down the empty hallway. My footfalls reverberated loudly, echoing all around as Larch's eerie thoughts chased after me, whispering inside my head: *Sleep tight, Svetlana.*

Three

I haven't always been a vampire—or at least I don't think so. It was only after we moved to Sunny Hill that I first began to realize it, that I began to change. Do you prefer to sleep under your bed? You might be a vampire, too.

I've read that vampires sleep in coffins. Do you think it's true? Are you a fool? Have you ever seen a coffin? They are extremely narrow—with a lid that closes down right over your face! Ridiculous! Do you like to roll over in your sleep? Well, so do I. The last thing I want is to wake up in the middle of the night and find that I can't roll over because I'm stuck in a silly coffin. What if I got a cramp? And not only that, anyone who saw the coffin would instantly know that I was a vampire—so how smart would that be? And can you imagine how freaked out my parents would be if I had a coffin in my room?

It's ludicrous.

I've already addressed the blood-drinking myth—ridiculous *ad infinitum*—which is Latin for "to the max."

Daylight? That's not a problem. Of course, I need to protect my eyes from harmful UV rays, same as everyone else, and I do use sunscreen, especially with my fair skin. The night, however, is when I am most powerful. My senses are perfectly attuned to the hours after the sun has fled. I see better in the dark than any cat. I can hear the slightest sounds. I can sense the *tap-tap-tapping* of cockroach legs creeping and the wiggle of worms burrowing deep beneath the ground. I can detect the flutter of a bat's wings high in the night sky and the scratching of tiny toenails as mice scurry across the cellar floor. In the black of night, I am supreme.

And with my first dreadful day at Sunny Hill Middle School behind me, the night couldn't come fast enough.

At the dinner table, I feasted on red peppers, red potatoes, tomato slices, and wild salmon (pink is red enough). When finished, I was eager to seek solace high in the branches of the Oak of Doom.

"May I be excused, please?"

"Don't you want some Jell-O before you run outside?" Dad asked.

"Is it red?"

"C'mon, Steph—I mean, Svetlana. A little green isn't going to kill you."

"Leave her alone," Mom said, coming to my defense. "She eats healthier than you or I do."

Dad hadn't entirely come to grips yet with my new diet. He dismissed my taste for red foods as attention-seeking behavior brought about by the family move from Texas to California. It was an interesting theory, but my taste buds weren't buying it.

"Is there any more of the red velvet cake left?" I wondered. My mother's red velvet cake is the best.

Unfortunately, her face relayed the bad news before her mouth ever moved. "I'm sorry." She shook her head, frowning, rolling her eyes toward my father. "Someone had the last piece already. And then that same someone had the nerve to make *green* Jell-O."

"Good job, Dad," I said, swallowing the sad fact that it would probably be weeks before Mom made my favorite dessert again. I'm usually reluctant to turn my vampiric powers on my parents, but I took a moment to plant the notion of strawberries and sponge cake into my mother's head for this coming weekend.

Dad widened his eyes in theatrical glee, guiding another jiggling spoonful of green Jell-O toward his mouth. "Mmm . . . delicious—it's so much better than red. You know, it wasn't that long ago that you thought green Jell-O was just fine, sweetie."

But not anymore, I thought. "Can I be excused?"

"You haven't said anything about how your classes went today," Mom observed, propping her chin onto her folded fingers and assuming her "tell me everything" pose.

"When I picked her up from school, she seemed awfully eager to leave," Dad noted.

Which was the understatement of the century. I couldn't get away from school fast enough. I shuddered, remembering the icy intrusion of Ms. Larch boring into my brain. How dare she! Also ... how *could* she? Only my formidable vampire skills had enabled me to break away and escape. What had she been probing my mind for? Did she know that I was a vampire? And most unsettling of all, what could I do about it? I had to go to school tomorrow—there was no way around that. Mom and Dad were both working now, and home-schooling was no longer an option. Could I somehow get out of going to Larch's science class? Or maybe attend an entirely different school altogether?

"What did you think, honey?" Mom asked. "Was school fun?"

"Fun is a word," I offered, tapping my knife impatiently against my empty plate.

"You're going to have to give it time, Stephanie," Dad advised, continuing to spoon wobbles of green jelly into his bowl.

"Svetlana!" I corrected. Was it so hard? Sss-vet-LAH-nah. Was it too much to ask?

His face reddened. "Svetlana—I'm sorry. And you know there's nothing wrong with the name Stephanie. It was perfectly fine for your grandmother. Before you know it, you're going to make all kinds of friends at school. You'll be in all sorts of clubs, and you can play sports or—" He verbally backpedaled away from my look of disgust. "Well, maybe not sports. But you can write for the school newspaper or join band or—"

"Just don't hate school right away," Mom suggested, reaching and stilling the clinking of my knife against the plate.

"Fine. I'll hate it next week." If I lasted until next week.

"Take it one day at a time," Dad suggested, brimming with unoriginality.

"Can I go, please?"

I dropped my dirty plate into the sink and laced up my black tennis shoes. Razor bolted between my legs as I opened the door, and we both rushed outside. In the far corner of the front yard, I climbed the ladder of boards up the Oak of Doom.

I wouldn't describe myself as an outdoors type, but when we first arrived in Sunny Hill, I insisted that Dad build me a private hangout in the largest tree in our front yard. He wasn't eager to do it, but a slight psychic push got the job done. I figured it was the least he could do since we'd left a perfectly wonderful life back in Texas just so he could make more money. I even tried to get my parents to allow me to sleep in my hangout overnight, but that was a definite no-go, at least for the time being. I didn't press it—you've got to pick your battles. That's Sun Tzu talking. He wrote the book on strategy, espionage, and war. Dad ended up not building my hangout as high up as I wanted, but it was high enough that I could easily see over the six-foot fence surrounding Morgloom Woods, which was basically our front and back yard.

Outside a window, I heard laughter and screaming coming from farther down Cherry Street. I spied through my binoculars and found Sandy Cross and her two minions, Marsha and Madison, bouncing like dodos on the trampoline in the front yard of the house on the corner. A smile crept across my face as I imagined one of them somersaulting off and splatting on the sidewalk. Am I bad? Please. My cousin in Texas has a trampoline. As I recall, the thrill lasted about two minutes. Why would anyone ever get on a trampoline twice? In my opinion, a trampoline is basically a Darwinian device for thinning the herd.

"Hey! What are you looking at?" a voice called from below.

I swung my binoculars down to the sidewalk beyond the fence and centered on Dwight Foote's round face staring up at me. I took the binoculars away and found Fumio Chen standing next to him.

"You spying on Sandy?" Foote asked.

"Of course not!" I lied, pointing vaguely into the air. "A kingfisher owl . . . just flew off thataway. You two must've spooked him—good job. It was the most magnificent specimen I've ever seen."

Foote shielded his thick glasses, looking around doubtfully. "I didn't see it."

"Hey, let us come up there!" Fumio shouted. The sun glinted brightly off his braces.

Come up here? Into my secret lair! What did Tweedledee and Tweedledum want? Nobody came up here—of course, I hadn't met anyone around here until today. But then, they weren't waiting for my permission, anyway. Fumio had unlatched the gate, and he and Foote were coming through. Razor rocketed across the yard, snapping and barking. He ran vicious circles around their feet, his black hotdog-shaped body racing like a cyclone.

Fumio bent down, grinning and wiggling his sausage

fingers, then jerked back as Razor snapped. "Whoa, doggie!"

"Don't move," I warned, dropping through the hole in the floor and scrambling down the ladder. I scooped Razor up off the ground. The yipping dachshund squirmed in my arms, barking fiercely. "Don't you have enough sense not to come barging through someone's gate? Doesn't 'Beware of Dog' mean anything to you?"

"Hey, chill out, Svetlana," Fumio suggested, jerking away as Razor unleashed a fresh barrage of barking.

"Get up the ladder, 'cause he's going back on the ground," I warned.

Razor growled and snapped around the bottom of the tree. I climbed after Fumio and Foote as they disappeared through the trapdoor.

"Cool," Foote said, rummaging around the tiny room. He picked up the slingshot I used for target shooting. I took it from him and placed it inside my trunk, closing the lid.

"Pretty lame books, though," Fumio said, lifting an Agatha Christie off the crate and tossing it aside.

"You boneheads obviously aren't familiar with Miss Manners," I observed.

"It's a cool tree house," Foote conceded, glancing admiringly around the room.

The hangout was pretty small; a single room with a window cut out of each side for a view in every direction. I'd tricked the space out with a trunk that I could padlock, shelves for books, and an overturned crate that functioned as a table. An old kitchen chair that my parents didn't use anymore was pushed against the wall, and Mom had stitched black curtains for the windows. I thought of the hangout more as an apartment than as a tree house, but I wasn't going to wrestle with Foote's limited experience.

Fumio stood at one of the windows, scanning Cherry Street with my binoculars. "You're definitely a spy, Svetlana." He focused on Sandy and her friends bouncing in the yard on the corner. "How come you never leave your yard?"

"Of course I leave the yard," I huffed, as if it was any of *his* business. I'd been out plenty—and all around the neighborhood. I'd ridden my bicycle to the mall and over to City Park. I'd taken the bus by myself to the downtown library. I'd been to the zoo and the museum. I knew the name on every mailbox as far as three streets over. I even knew where Fumio Chen lived. "If I don't leave the yard, then how do I know you live over on Stallings Street in the house with the silver gazing ball in the yard? Which, by the way, is extremely tacky."

"'Cause you're a spy," he said, proving his point.

Clever. "Sun Tzu prescribes knowing one's enemy," I countered, grabbing my binoculars from him and setting them down on the table. "Now, what do you *boys* want?"

"Sun who?" Foote scratched his big head.

"He wrote *The Art of War*," Fumio explained.

I was impressed but not swayed.

"So what do you do up here in this place anyway—besides spy?" Foote wondered. He slid against the wall down to the floor and sat with his legs crossed Indian-style.

"Make yourself comfortable," I said, dripping sarcasm.

Fumio said, "All right, ice queen, we get it—you're tough. But just try relaxing and being a bit friendly—just so you can say you did it once. I'm sure being nice won't agree with you, but at least you'll have had the experience." He finished his amateur assessment, planting his butt in my chair.

I gave him the thumb. "Out, brace-face."

"Very original. You're like a genius." But he got up and slid down to the floor beside Foote.

I pushed my chair away and sat.

"What do *you two* do around here?" I asked, turning the table on their interrogation.

"Lots," Fumio said. "For one, I'm a reporter for the school paper, the *Sunny Hill Bee*." He knelt up and pulled a notebook from the back pocket of his jeans. "And Dwight takes photos."

Foote slid a digital camera from a holster on his belt. "It's got seven megapixels and a 5X zoom, and I can record videos with sound." He clicked a button on the camera, and it whirred to life.

"Don't—" I started, but the flash went off in my face. I rubbed at the stars dancing before my eyes. "Jerk. If you want that camera thrown out the window, just take another picture."

"Check it out." Foote shoved the camera in my face so I could view an image of myself lifting my hands up to block the shot.

What? You thought a vampire couldn't be photographed? That a vampire can't cast a reflection? Wrong. Vampires are subject to the same physical laws that rule every creature. The things that make a vampire a vampire are the brain and the heart. A vampire brain is vastly superior to an ordinary individual's brain. That's why my senses are so keenly developed. And a vampire heart can never be defeated.

I pushed aside the camera and told Foote to get out of my face.

"I've got an idea," Fumio said. He tapped a pen against his notebook. "I think your tree house might make an interesting story for the paper—kind of a 'get to know the new girl in school' piece. Dwight can take some shots of you standing at the window, and I'll write up a little—"

"No way," I protested, experiencing a surge of panic as extreme as the one Ms. Larch had brought on at the end of science class. "You do that and you're both dead. And I'm completely serious."

"Whoa, Svetlana, most kids would kill to be in the school paper—not to stay out of it. What's the big deal?" Fumio sensed my distress, enjoying it. He planted a fat smile across his face.

Not a smart move.

I pulled him roughly from the floor. Before he could react, I had him pushed halfway out the nearest window. The smile fled from his face, and he hollered in panic. He grasped desperately for the window frame. I gripped his shirt collar and heaved. He grabbed at my wrists and then at the fluttering curtains. I bent him farther backward across the windowsill.

"Whoa! Whoa! Pull me back!"

He swatted at my face, flailing his arms. I shook him

at the end of my bunched fists. Put me in the school paper, would he? I'd drop him on his head. "You write one little word, or put one little picture of me in your loser *Bee,* and I'll bury you." I clenched my teeth, gritting over his terrified face.

Foote tapped gently on my shoulder. "We could do a fluff piece about Principal Talbot's cat instead," he offered.

I dragged Fumio back inside.

He straightened his wrinkled collar, coughing, his eyes watering as he smoothed his shirtfront. "You—you could have dropped me!"

Foote patted him on the back and told him that maybe they should pass on the tree house story. I realized Dwight Foote might have more going on inside that big head of his than I'd given him credit for.

"No story," I said.

"No story. Geez . . ." Fumio twisted his neck from side to side. "You could've messed up my vertebrates, man."

I suddenly had an idea of my own. "If you want to do a story on somebody, why not write an exposé about Ms. Larch—she's new, right?" I figured that this might be an opportunity for me to learn more about the creepy science teacher who wanted to cram an apple down my throat.

Foote shook his head and said, "We already did a story on her in last month's edition."

"Yeah," Fumio croaked. "Right after she took over Mr. Boyd's class."

"Mr. Boyd was the science teacher who disappeared, right?"

"That's right," Foote said. "There's a rumor he skipped town to escape the FBI."

"For bank robbery," Fumio added. "He was a sharp dresser and drove a fast car—a canary-yellow Corvette—which is a little more car than most of the lame teachers at Sunny Hill Middle can handle."

"So where did Ms. Larch come from?"

"She moved here from England," Fumio answered, scrunching up his face in thought. He counted off on his fingers. "She has a dog named Sparky, her favorite food is pizza, she hates violence on TV, and she loves jazz."

"You're quite the muckraker," I said, tapping the tip of my finger to the end of my nose. "No husband or children?"

"Nope."

"Have you noticed anything at all strange about her? Or heard anyone saying anything weird about her?"

"Well, er, no. . . . Like what?" Fumio looked from Foote to me, wondering what I was getting at.

"Nothing," I said. I needed to find out more about Ms. Larch, but what I really wanted to know wasn't going to be in the pages of the *Sunny Hill Bee*.

"Do you know the Bone Lady next door?" Foote asked. He'd picked up my binoculars from the table and was aiming them out the window.

"No," I answered, stepping up and taking them from his hands. I looked to the brick house where Lenora Bones had recently taken up residence. Scanning with the binoculars, I finally found my neighbor's face in a second-floor window, staring back through binoculars of her own. She lowered her spyglasses and winked.

What the heck was going on here?

The old woman smiled and waved, then stepped back from the window. Dark curtains dropped, and she was gone.

It seemed I wasn't the only spy in the neighborhood.

Four

Six months ago, when we first moved from Texas to Sunny Hill, California, I couldn't sleep. At first, I thought it was simply the nervousness of starting a new life, the excitement of being in a new place and living in a new house. But weeks passed, and I still couldn't get through the night without tossing and turning. Often I stayed awake all night, watching shadows play across the ceiling. I listened to the ticking of the grandfather clock downstairs and the gurgle of water pouring through pipes hidden in the walls and the beating of moth wings against the window. It seemed that I noticed every little sound. I tried wrapping my pillow around my head to block out the noises that were once little but now deafeningly loud, but it didn't help.

My mother was worried because I looked tired all the time. Black circles appeared under my eyes. I lost my appetite. I didn't enjoy eating anymore. My favorite food—bananas—tasted awful. Broccoli had always been bad, but now it was worse. I despised carrot cake. I hated hot chocolate. Orange juice made me irritable. I loathed lemon bars and blueberries and green peas. Even Neapolitan ice cream made me gag—or at least the chocolate part did. I liked the strawberry part. And I didn't mind the vanilla. And I didn't mind spaghetti or lasagna or ravioli—or any kind of pasta, so long as it was buried in tomato sauce. I didn't mind a rare hamburger with loads of ketchup. Or red cabbage stew. Or red beans and rice. Or red snapper with a red pepper sauce and a sprinkling of paprika. Or anything red, really.

So I ate red foods and felt better.

And then I began sleeping under my bed.

You wouldn't think it was comfortable, but I slept like a baby. Each night, after I finished reading, I'd snap off the light and crawl under the bed with my blanket, and sleep the sleep of the dead. Or the undead. It was as if I fell into a deep coma where my newly sensitive senses could find respite.

Until last night.

Now I found myself tossing and turning once more, but this time with the nightmarish red fingernails of Ms. Larch clutching at me in sleep. When the alarm clock buzzed in the morning, I jerked awake from fitful sleep, banging my head on the wooden brace underneath the bed. "Good grief," I grumbled aloud, rubbing the knot already rising on my noggin. It was not a great way to start the day.

"You sure you don't want me to take you to school again this morning?" Dad asked, looking up from the sports scores in the newspaper.

"It's only a ten-minute pedal away," I assured him. I'd decided to ride my bicycle.

Mom had already left to substitute at the high school, and Dad would be leaving soon to do whatever a business systems analyst did. I finished my strawberry yogurt, grabbed my lunch box and school bag, and collected my bike from the garage.

The sun was barely up over the rooftops along Cherry Street. I coasted down the driveway and pedaled slowly past the house next door. Long shadows thrown by twisted trees fell across the yard, climbing up the brick walls of the Bone Lady's house. Black curtains were drawn closed. Did one of the curtains move at the upstairs window in the corner? Silver letters on the black mailbox spelled out the name Lenora Bones.

A sudden squeaking came from behind. I was startled by the shrill ringing of bells and a loud clatter as three bicycles sped past, almost knocking me over. I wobbled on my bike, losing my balance. I had to drop a foot to the street to keep from crashing. Goons!

Sandy Cross and her entourage pedaled past, yipping and squealing. "C'mon, Stephanie!" they cried. "C'mon, slowpoke, you're gonna be late!"

Imbeciles. Excessive trampolining had obviously scrambled their bird-sized brains. I steadied myself and followed slowly after their shrinking shapes. I glanced once more over my shoulder at the Bone Lady's house. At the corner window, an edge of black curtain was pulled aside slightly, as if someone were peeking from the shadows.

I made it to school with time to spare. In Mr. Dumloch's class, sitting at my desk behind Sandy Cross, I fought the urge to reach into her mass of blond hair and thump her on her ear.

The stink of Dumpy Dumloch's cologne did little to improve my mood. He wallowed behind his desk, following his finger down the roll, calling names. "Dwight Foote?"

"Here," Foote answered, stretching his response into a yawn. His mouth opened into a cavern in the middle of his giant face. Would it be too much for him to put a hand over that hole? Were these kids raised in barns?

Fumio Chen tapped the back of my head with a rolled-up paper. "Here's a copy of last month's *Sunny Hill Bee*," he said, handing it to me. "Larch is on page three."

There were only four pages.

Class began and I put the paper aside for later. Dumloch, impossibly, was even more boring than he'd been yesterday. How could one man make the history of the *entire world* boring? Math was a little better—and the instructor, Mrs. Fry, definitely had a glass eye. She blinked, but the brown marble never moved. Gym class was—as it forever would be—unbearable. My legs really are too white for public display—gorgeous, but too white. And did I really need to get all hot and sweaty in gym class right before lunch? Also, I'm pretty sure it's universally accepted within the medical community that sit-ups are actually not the best thing for your spine. Unfortunately,

Coach Cooper (who smells like cigarettes) wasn't privy to that information. She also seemed entirely disinterested in anything I had to offer on the subject.

Lunch couldn't come fast enough.

Today, I'd packed fruit punch, raspberry jam on white bread, watermelon squares, and two sticks of red licorice. I took a seat at one of the long cafeteria tables and poked my drinking straw into the fruit-punch box. I unrolled the school newspaper Fumio had given me in first period. Beside me, Dwight Foote dropped his tray of food onto the table and clumsily plopped onto the bench. His elbow jostled my hand, and I dribbled fruit punch down my wrist. I bit back a curse, scowling.

"What's up, Svetlana?" He smiled lamely behind his thick eyeglasses. *Blink. Blink.*

I slid away. "Are you familiar with the concept of *personal space,* Foote? Are you trying to get on my bad side?"

"You're kidding, right? You don't even have a good side. I think you're antisocial or something."

"You know, your opinion would mean so much more if I didn't have to look at the macaroni in your mouth while you expressed it."

He closed his mouth, chewing with a frown.

"Your potential is appreciated," I informed him.

The cafeteria tables filled up as everyone in first lunch collected their meals and took a seat. Banners on the walls cried victory for the Sunny Hill Spartans. A poster announced the Spring Fling Carnival coming this weekend. Mr. Dumloch waddled through the busy room carrying a sack lunch. He disappeared behind a swinging door marked TEACHER LOUNGE. Three tables over, I spied the back of Sandy Cross's blond head bobbing between her two minions, Marsha and Madison.

I returned my attention to the school newspaper and found the story regarding Ms. Larch. There was a grainy black-and-white photo of her standing next to the flagpole at the front of the school. The headline read "Sunny Hill Welcomes Ms. Larch" and below that was Fumio Chen's name followed by two paragraphs describing how excited Ms. Larch was to be a part of Sunny Hill Middle School and how much she looked forward to working with the faculty and students. Chen's hard-hitting exposé not only revealed her favorite food and the name of her dog, it also uncovered the fact that her astrological sign was Pisces. *Great job, Fumio.* As I neared the end of the article, an electric tingling tickled down my spine, and my nose filled with the scent of spoiled food. I looked up.

"That's not a very good picture of me, is it?" Ms. Larch whispered, reaching across my shoulder and tapping a long red fingernail on the page. "Couldn't you have taken a better photograph than that, Dwight?" she asked.

Beside me, Dwight Foote garbled, "It was a good picture; it just didn't print well." His mouth was crammed with fried chicken now.

"Please chew with your mouth closed, Dwight," she suggested.

Ms. Larch leaned down so that her face was only inches from my own. Her cherry-candy-flavored breath blew in my face. "Does the story interest you, Svetlana?"

She lifted her hand from the paper and rested it on my shoulder.

I pulled away.

Foote said, "Fumio wanted to do a story on Svetlana, and she nearly threw him out a window." He laughed and nudged at me annoyingly with his elbow.

"You don't want to be in the school paper, Svetlana?" Ms. Larch asked, feigning curiosity. "Don't you want everyone to know who you are?"

Who I am? What did she know about who I was?

Her nails pressed for a moment, menacingly, into my shoulder. She stood straight and patted me gently. "Enjoy your lunch." She reached and plucked a cube of watermelon from my plastic tub. "You don't mind, do you?" She closed her red lips around it. "It's one of my favorites."

She winked and walked away. Something in the way she moved made me think of a cat—and not a tame tabby but a stalking tiger or lioness. She didn't walk so much as glide across the cafeteria floor. Her fire-engine-red dress clung like Christmas wrapping paper, and her hips tick-tocked like the pendulum of a clock. She looked more like a movie star than a sixth-grade science teacher—even if she did smell like garbage.

"Does she always stink like that?" I asked Foote.

"Like what?"

"Are you kidding? Does your nose even work? That woman smells like garbage. Ms. Larch needs to be taken out to the curb." I thought the remark was pretty clever, but Foote looked at me as if he didn't get it. "You don't smell her?"

"What?"

I couldn't believe it. He didn't have a clue. As big as Foote's nose was on that basketball-sized head of his, he obviously didn't suffer the aromatic bite wafting off Sylvia Larch. I watched her disappear through the teacher lounge door.

Did Ms. Larch know I was a vampire? And was she one herself? Did she sleep under her bed and eat only foods that were red? Yesterday, she'd probed my thoughts and laughed over my disdain of chocolate. She'd poured her syrupy voice into my head: *Sweet Svetlana, I know who you are.* She had antagonized me with the red apple, confronted me by shoving it in my face. What did she know?

Later in the afternoon, in science, Ms. Larch offered no more chocolate treats. She stank to high heaven, riper today than yesterday. The rot smell now was even worse than it had been in the cafeteria. The class lesson was about decomposition, about the breakdown of tissues, which seemed fitting. "Decomposition," she said, "begins at the instant of death."

She sure loved the subject. She said lots of stuff about worms and flies, smiling all the while. When the final bell rang, everyone hastily gathered up their materials and rushed out into the hallway.

I collected my books and approached the teacher's desk just as the last kid banged out the door. Ms. Larch's glinting green eyes followed me with amusement. I wondered if this was what a mouse saw when it came upon a cat.

"Ms. Larch?"

She steepled her slender fingers beneath her chin.

"Yes, Svetlana?" Her red mouth curled at the corners.

I concentrated, forming the words in my mind. *Can you hear me?* I thought, directing my words into her head.

Her eyes went wide in slight amusement. "Of course I can hear you," she replied.

I knew it was real, but there was still a part of me that didn't believe it could be happening. I stood frozen before her desk.

She laughed.

Had I thought that I'd only imagined her words in my mind yesterday? Was this really possible? *Are you . . . like me?* I spilled the question without thinking, and suddenly found myself quivering in anticipation, hanging on the answer.

"Like you?" The expression over her face turned quizzical. She reached and tapped a red fingernail to her lips. Her green eyes sparkled, amused. "And what . . . are you like, Svetlana?"

"A . . . vampire?" I whispered.

For a moment, her face showed no expression whatsoever, then she dissolved into quiet giggling. I waited for her to stop, but she didn't. She kept laughing, covering her mouth and giggling through her fingers. She began slapping her desk, and soon her giggles grew louder, turning to guffaws. She wrapped her arms about herself and laughed and laughed. Her eyes watered, and tears began streaming down her face. She pounded the desk with her fist and gulped for air and pointed and laughed.

She was still laughing when I left.

I pedaled home with my teeth clenched and my cheeks burning.

Five

The Bone Lady interrupted our dinner with a plateful of cookies.

The knocking came as a sandpapery-soft whisper at the front door. Mom put down her soupspoon and stepped away to investigate. She returned a moment later with our elderly neighbor in tow.

"Oh, please, don't let me disturb your meal!" Lenora Bones exclaimed, shuffling into the dining room, bringing with her a cloud of scrumptious-cookie aroma. She clutched a tinfoil-wrapped plate in her spidery hands. The emaciated old lady couldn't have been more aptly named; she was nothing but thin skin stretched over a tiny skeleton. She stood slightly stooped, barely rising to the height of my mother's shoulder.

Mom introduced Dad and me.

"Oh, yes, I've seen you playing with that energetic

dog of yours, young lady," Lenora Bones said brightly. Her eyes, wet and shiny, were as gray as storm clouds.

"Please join us for dinner," Mom invited.

"Oh, no, I couldn't. But thank you. I wanted to stop by sooner and say hello, but with cleaning and unpacking and settling in—so much work—I just haven't found time until now. I finally got around to baking cookies and thought it might provide a good excuse to drop by and introduce myself." She set the covered plate on the table. Her knotted fingers were like thin twigs; the skin on her hands was veined and spotted. "It's only a few sugar cookies."

Mother pulled a chair from the table and insisted Ms. Bones take a seat.

"Well, I feel just awful intruding. . . ." The older woman looked around, embarrassed, but let herself be seated.

"Don't be silly," Mom assured, snapping her fingers and pointing me to the kitchen. "I've been meaning to knock on your door and say hello."

I went into the kitchen and returned a moment later with a bowl of soup.

"Tomato soup! My favorite!" Our wrinkled neighbor clapped her hands with pleasure. "Thank you so much, Svetlana, it's wonderful. And such a beautiful name!" She reached out quickly and grabbed my hand. She squeezed with more strength than I would have thought her capable of.

"Well," Dad began, clearing his throat. "Stephanie has only recently become fixated on the name Svetlana. She's actually named after my mother, who—"

"Oh, Svetlana is an excellent name!" Ms. Bones interrupted, nodding with vigor. "Very exotic—very mysterious . . . and strong! I believe that everyone should choose his or her own name. Of course, Bones is the perfect name for me!" The old woman chuckled, unfolding a paper napkin and stuffing a corner of it into the high neck of her black dress. "Would you believe my father actually named me Sheila? Oh, I'm not a Sheila at all!" She winked at me and tapped the brim of her bowl with her silver spoon. She ladled up a spoonful of steaming soup and blew across it. "This looks lovely."

"Where have you recently moved from, Ms. Bones?" Mom asked.

"Anyone who feeds me dinner must call me Lenora, am I right? And London, England, was my previous address." *Slurp. Slurp.* "Such wonderful soup! But I've been a bit of a tramp since retiring. I've lived here and there and everywhere: Australia and China and the lower parts of Peru—I can no longer take the thin air in the mountains, unfortunately. I've lived in almost every corner of Africa—quite a place that is. Nice and hot."

"And you're retired?" Dad wondered.

"From teaching," she answered, blowing and slurping. "Delicious."

"I've just returned to teaching myself," Mom explained. "Substituting—until a permanent position opens."

"That's wonderful," Ms. Bones said. "I never did tire of teaching, you know. Or of the children. Or learning. Which might be something Svetlana could lend me a hand with." The old lady swiveled her thin-skinned skull around, fixing me with shiny eyes. "Do you enjoy reading, Svetlana?"

"She reads more than anyone in this house," Mom announced with pride.

"I do like to read," I boasted.

"Of course you do," Lenora Bones agreed. "What intelligent person doesn't? But these tired eyes of mine can't keep up with my appetite! I simply cannot read like I used to—or wish to still. I've got a proposition for you—if you're interested and if your kind parents will allow it." She wrapped her skeletal fingers around my mother's hand. "I had a lovely neighbor girl in London whom I employed to read to me—only a small wage and a few hours a week. It would be so nice if I could continue to do that here." She threw up her hands. "So now I'm discovered! I thought I'd break in with a plate of cookies and see if I couldn't sway you!" Lenora Bones went wide-eyed at her confession, smiling from face to face around the table.

What was she saying? She wanted to pay me to read to her? That sounded too good to be true. What books would she have me read? Charles Dickens or Emily Brontë, I'd bet.

"Well, that would be fine with me," I said, looking from Mom to Dad, shrugging and grinning. Should I ask how much she wanted to pay me? Would that be rude? What if it was something ridiculous, like fifty cents an hour? She had to be at least seventy years old, maybe even eighty. Old people had funny ideas about money. Like Dad's mom, the grandma I was named after. She was a little daffy, always going on about how much everything costs nowadays. Who knew what this old woman was thinking?

"I think that would be fine, Ms. Bones—" Mom started.

"Lenora!" the old woman insisted.

"Lenora. But I don't know if Svetlana needs to be paid."

What? I swung my leg under the table to kick Mom but missed.

"If it's only a couple of hours a week, I'm sure she'd enjoy doing it for fun. Right, honey?" Mom was nodding at me, smiling.

Was Mom out of her mind? The old lady wanted to pay me! It would probably make her feel better if she did.

"Oh, no, I would have to pay a little something for her efforts," Ms. Bones insisted. "It'd make me feel better if I did." The old woman winked and reached over to pat the top of my hand.

Dad cleared his throat. "I think that would be a good thing, don't you, Svetlana?" He was solid on the *Svetlana*.

"Sure . . ."

"Terrific." Lenora Bones scraped a last spoonful of soup from her bowl and swallowed it with a wet slurp. "I'm already looking forward to it."

We decided on Saturday afternoon. Ms. Bones thanked Mom and Dad profusely for dinner and rose shakily from the table. As the joints in her knees and hips popped like splintering wood, she let her mouth fall open into a shocked "O." "Ouch," she joked, widening her eyes

41

in mock surprise. "A body at rest tends to remain at rest—especially this old body of mine." She winked.

When Mom returned to the table after seeing Ms. Bones out the door, she said, "That old gal's got a lot of personality."

"Uh-huh," Dad agreed.

"I believe you'll have a terrific time reading to her," Mom told me. "You're sweet to do it, and I'm very proud of you." She stooped and gave me a squeeze. "Shall we try milk and cookies for dessert?"

It sounded like a good idea to me. The fresh-baked aroma escaping from the old woman's plate filled every corner of the room. Mom peeled the foil covering from the serving dish, revealing a mound of circle-shaped red cookies.

"Well, take a look at that," Dad said, reaching and grabbing one. "Just the way you like them, Steph—Svetlana."

Six

On Wednesday, Dwight Foote was absent from school. But the following day, he was back in Dumloch's class for first period. His left arm was in a cast from thumb to elbow and strapped in a sling across his waist.

"What happened to you?" I asked.

Sandy Cross turned around in her seat, glaring at Foote. Her mouth was scrunched up as if she'd bitten into a lemon. Baubles of garish pink plastic dangled from her earlobes. Were those little legs hanging off her earrings? Were they ladybugs?

"Ask *her*," Foote said, pointing his good thumb in Sandy's direction.

"My father's taking down my trampoline because of you!" Sandy complained in a huff. Her insect earrings trembled with displeasure.

"You should have seen it." Fumio Chen laughed behind me. "Dwight flew off the trampoline—and right onto the sidewalk."

"It wasn't funny at the time," Foote murmured. "I could've broken my camera."

"It's not funny *now,*" Sandy said, bunching up her face. "Nobody invited you onto my trampoline, anyhow."

"I swear," Fumio chuckled. "He landed on his head and broke his arm. I can't explain it."

"I cracked my radius bone straight through." Foote traced a finger down his cast. "Sandy's dad's gotta pay for it or my dad's gonna sue her family into the dirt."

"You're a moron!" Sandy cried.

"All right, settle down," Dumloch demanded, waddling up and down the aisles, trailing cheap cologne and setting a ten-question pop quiz on each student's desktop. "Eyes straight ahead, and you've got fifteen minutes."

The class gave a collective groan. Dumloch trundled back behind his desk and sat, staring up at the ceiling, chewing the paint off a pencil with his awful teeth. Despite his distracted gnawing, I finished the test in less than five minutes with a perfect score. Public school was a heck of a lot easier than my mom's home-schooling.

The morning crept along, and by lunch I was starving. Dwight Foote joined me in the cafeteria. He indicated the cast on his arm and asked if I'd cut up his chicken-fried steak for him.

"Good grief," I breathed, setting my tomato sandwich aside and sawing his meat into eight pieces.

"Thanks, Svet. Do you mind if I call—"

"I definitely *do* mind." What was I, a pet?

44

"Well . . . thanks, Svetlana." *Blink. Blink.* He shoved meat and gravy into his mouth, making cow eyes at me.

Across the cafeteria, Ms. Larch followed Dumloch through the swinging door into the teacher lounge. Sandy Cross stalked by, throwing Foote a menacing glare and me a not much better one, which was fine with me. She sat at the next table over with her back to us and was joined shortly by Madison and Marsha, each glancing daggers in our direction. All three girls wore the same hideous ladybug-shaped earrings. I half-heard their giggling and complaining. Their trilling brought to mind a nest of begging baby birds. These were the cool kids? I'd thought that MTV and the Disney Channel had prepared me for the lameness of school, but I was colossally unprepared.

The school day crept like molasses.

Later, in science class, Ms. Larch appeared wholly uninterested in teaching. The stench of rotten garbage was so strong, I could hardly concentrate on her lecture. "What is that awful smell?" I whispered to Foote, but he didn't know what I was talking about. Perhaps he *had* bounced on his head yesterday. Nobody else in class seemed disturbed by the odor. Behind her desk, the science teacher droned on, looking haggard and tired. At one point, she caught me staring, and her eyes narrowed into mean slits.

What are you gawking at!

Her invading voice erupted in my head, making me jump in my seat. Nobody else heard. Larch continued to look unhappy and distracted, even as a smile spread across her face at my obvious discomfort. Halfway through class, she ceased lecturing, popped in a documentary, and hurried from the room, as if she were about to be sick.

Foote leaned over and whispered, "I thought she was gonna blow chunks."

When the final bell of the day rang, the film (hyenas and their tenuous coexistence with lions) was still playing. Ms. Larch had yet to return to the classroom. Everyone looked about, uncertain what to do. I got up and hit the lights, and everyone scrambled for their belongings, bolting to freedom.

Lemmings, I thought.

Seven

Have you ever known a person who thinks she's *it on a stick?* The *center of the universe?* Someone who seems to never have any doubts. Who acts as if she's always right (when she's almost always wrong!)? A person who believes she's the most beautiful (hardly!) and the smartest (right!). Someone who annoys you right down to the bone—simply by breathing?

What do you do with someone like that? I remember reading somewhere that the things you find to criticize in others are really the things you wish to improve in yourself. I wouldn't discount the idea. I'm a student of the human condition. I'm aware that my social skills need a lot of work, and I'm far from perfect. Still, when I'm around a girl like that—someone like Sandy Cross—I just want to punch her in the nose.

I was unlocking my bicycle from the bike rack after school. Sandy and her minions were there as well.

"Why do you dress like you're going to a funeral?" Sandy asked from across the rack. Her wannabe-clever mouth labored around *at least* three gobs of sugar-soaked bubblegum.

Is wearing black a crime? What was the big deal? I like black! It's very slimming.

Next to Sandy, Madison pulled away the chain that locked her and Sandy's and Marsha's bicycles together, the links rattling over steel. "She dresses like she's the one being buried," Madison quipped.

"You know that's not a Goth look, right?" Marsha said, eyeing me critically from head to toe. "You don't have enough eye makeup on. You need to wear heavier boots, and wristbands with metal studs—a collar, maybe. You need a fat black belt, too. You need more silver."

"No," Madison disagreed. "That's the Metal look."

"It's Goth."

"What we're *trying* to say," Sandy interjected, blowing and popping a pink bubble, "is that you need help."

Could these three possibly be serious? I took the U-lock off my bicycle and tossed it into the front basket with my book bag. What could I say to these bimbos? "You're wearing matching earrings," I noted. Did they think that was cool? Did their parents dress them? "You have pink plastic bugs dangling from your ears."

"We're not trying to fight with you, okay?" Sandy said. "And we're not trying to put you down, either." She pulled a string of blond hair away from the corner of her mouth and continued chomping her bubblegum. *Smack. Smack. Smack.*

"So lighten up, Metalhead," Madison told me.

"And chill out," Marsha added.

The two beanpole girls pushed their bikes toward the sidewalk.

Sandy guided her bicycle around the rack next to mine. "You know, we wouldn't even talk to you if we didn't think you were all right, okay?"

Smooth—the old switcheroo. Now *I* was the jerk. Well, that was fine. Mostly I just wanted to be left alone. "Whatever," I said.

"If you want to go to the mall with us, you're invited," she said out of the blue, arching a sculpted brow over her left eye. "You can even hang with us at the Spring Fling Carnival this weekend—if you're not too cool for that. What do you say, Stephanie?"

A challenge.

Stephanie.

"That's not my name," I whispered.

"Well, would *Svetlana* care to hang out?"

Marsha and Madison waited on the sidewalk with twig-like arms crossed, leaning against their bikes.

Right.

"No, thanks," I said. Surprisingly, the idea wasn't completely unappealing, but what could I really do with these Barbie clones? Look at clothes? I didn't have any money anyhow.

"If you want to be the Lone Ranger, that's up to you," Sandy said, shrugging and pushing her bike away. "But you're getting a little old to be playing in a tree house, and you're not gonna have my trampoline to spy on anymore."

The three girls climbed onto their bikes. One of the twins, I couldn't tell which, shouted, "Later, Lame-o!"

Sandy laughed, tossing back her mop of straw hair. She pedaled away, screaming, "See you tomorrow, Stephanie!"

But she was dead wrong.

Eight

Nobody thought much of it when Sandy was missing from Mr. Dumloch's class the next morning. Her desk sat empty as Dumloch mummified us into a state of complete boredom with his bland regurgitation of Egyptian history. He plodded up and down the rows of desks trailing an eye-burning cloud of aftershave, droning on like a dying fan, but far less interesting.

"You've gotta smell *that*, right?" I whispered to Foote, holding my nose after Dumloch had passed.

Dwight stuck his finger down his throat in a gagging gesture.

Fumio leaned forward and whispered, "He must bathe in the stuff."

"What was that, Mr. Chen?" Dumloch asked, rotating his rotund body.

"I said 'Those pharaohs sure had it tough,' sir."

"I'm sure you did," Dumloch said, eyeing Fumio with obvious doubt. He went behind his desk and dropped into his chair. He smiled strangely at me over Sandy's empty desk. Without her annoying explosion of blond hair to hide behind, his beady eyes bored directly into me from the doughy folds of his face. I could hardly believe it, but I actually wished Sandy Cross were in class.

Dumloch said, "I think history should be tough, too, so I think we'll have another pop quiz today."

Grumbling rippled through the classroom.

Gym class wasn't any better; the sit-ups were getting out of hand. I was obviously going to have to Google and print out some data for Coach Cooper. Didn't she realize the damage sit-ups inflicted upon our still young and developing bodies? A classmate sat on my feet as I was forced to curl into thirty painful sit-ups. Alison Finch, redheaded and sporting a billion freckles, held my legs and counted as I groaned through the crunches.

"Twenty-one, twenty-eight, twenty-nine . . . and thirty," she called.

At least my gym partner had some sense. Between the two of us, we managed to short Coach ten lashes. I thought the purpose of gym class was physical fitness. The popping in my spine said otherwise.

As I limped from the gym to the cafeteria, I passed two police cars parked in front of the school office. Some of the kids inside the cafeteria were hanging around the windows staring out at the cruisers.

"What do you think that's about?" I asked Foote as he took his seat.

"Beats me," he said, focusing on drawing mustard stripes across his meatloaf.

Today, I'd brought bologna on white bread (extra mayo) along with a cup of cherry tomatoes, some cranberry juice, and three of the sugar cookies Lenora Bones had baked (delicious!). I cut the crusts from my sandwich and watched the kids who were lined up along the windows staring outside. I didn't see the beanpole twins, Marsha and Madison, anywhere which kind of made sense, since they were surgically attached to Sandy Cross.

"What do you think Sandy and her robots are up to today?"

"Who cares," Foote said. "Something stupid, no doubt."

Everyone in the room quieted, and the kids at the windows took their seats as Principal Talbot led two uniformed police officers through the cafeteria and into the teacher lounge. When the swinging door closed after them, the room erupted into a murmuring buzz.

"I bet it's about Mr. Boyd," Foote decided. "The authorities probably caught up with him or got a hot lead."

But that wasn't the case. After lunch, Fumio Chen found us in the hallway and told us that the cops were actually looking for the three girls. "What I know is this," he said, taking a deep breath. "Tony Cassini was in the office seeing the school nurse because of his messed-up breathing, and he heard Mrs. Stiles tell Mrs. Fry that she needed to report pronto to the teacher lounge because the cops were asking all the teachers questions about Sandy and Marsha and Madison because they never got home from school yesterday." He finally sucked another breath into his beet-red face.

The girls never got home yesterday? "Are you saying they're missing?" I asked.

"I don't know—I'm just saying what Tony said."

And by last period, everyone in school knew what Tony had said.

Ms. Larch rapped a ruler across the top of her desk as the bell rang for the start of class, but kids continued to whisper. "Be quiet now," she told everyone, rapping louder.

Her lips were painted in rich red. She seemed somehow taller today. I glanced down the length of her sleek black dress to her stiletto sandals and crimson toenails. A silver toe-ring wrapped the littlest toe on her right foot. Her face was flush with color, like a rose. She glowed with vigor—not at all like yesterday, when she'd been sickly and seemingly on the verge of throwing up. She surveyed the class slowly, finally settling her eyes on me, letting the look linger. I tensed, half expecting her voice to blossom inside my mind, but she only smiled and looked away.

"It's time to shut down the rumor mill and begin class. I know everyone is buzzing with gossip, but I'm certain the authorities would rather we did otherwise." Ms. Larch lifted the science text and instructed us all to turn to worms on page ninety-seven.

Did you know that the largest earthworm ever found was twenty-two feet long? Does anyone need to know this? I wasn't the least unhappy when the final bell brought an end to *Lumbricus terrestris*.

"Svetlana, a moment, please," Ms. Larch said after class.

The rest of the kids filed into the hallway while I waited nervously before the teacher's desk, clutching my book bag in hand. The classroom door closed with a hollow click after the last student. Larch drummed painted nails on the desktop. Her other hand was propped beneath the point of her chin, her index finger tapping thoughtfully over smiling lips.

"Your father's not picking you up today?"

"I rode my bicycle."

"I've never ridden a bicycle," she said. *Am I missing anything?*

The question was asked after her lips had ceased moving. There was something soothing in the way the words whispered to life behind my eyes.

How do you do that? I thought. And asked, without thinking.

The corners of her mouth curled toward her eyes. *How do* you *do it?* Her emerald eyes laughed.

Did I hear her laughter inside my head?

I stood with my book bag clutched to my chest. I stared and found myself falling into the swirling greenness of her eyes. It was as if I was tumbling from a great height toward a frothing sea far below. I reached for the edge of the desk and steadied myself. Was there music in my head? A gentle piping?

Have you ever spoken in thoughts to anyone else? she asked. *Have the thoughts of another ever come to you, Svetlana?*

I felt the words in my mind, but something else, too,

like a hand feeling its way in the dark, rummaging through an unfamiliar drawer. Ms. Larch was in my mind, searching. I forced myself to look away, and the feeling evaporated.

"Very good," she said, her smile dissolving into something unreadable. "You can protect yourself. But you have nothing to fear from me. I'm your friend, Svetlana."

"I'm . . ." I didn't know what I wanted to say. I was suddenly dizzy.

Ms. Larch chuckled and came around the desk and stood very close. She searched my eyes, lowering her face to mine. Cherry breath blew from her lips. I detected the clicking of a lozenge against her perfect teeth. The unpleasant rot of rancid meat was still there, but only slightly, perhaps only a memory.

"The other day," she said. "Why did you say to me what you did? That you were a vampire?"

"I . . ."

Is it because of this? The sharing of thoughts? And the taste of red?

"You're the same," I said. "You only eat what's red."

Her lips peeled back in a serpent smile. "Most certainly red," she breathed.

"And do you sleep under your bed?"

The question seemed to surprise her. "Under my bed?" A puzzled expression settled on her face. "You sleep under your bed?"

"Yes."

"Well, I don't know what that's about."

"We're the same," I said. "Vampires."

Ms. Larch touched my cheek, the icy smoothness of her palm stingingly cold against my bare skin. I flinched from her touch and the slight scent of something spoiled.

"Svetlana," she whispered, "there's no such thing as vampires."

Gentle laughter seeped into my thoughts, like the soft ringing of a wind chime; tinkling petals of thin steel between my ears.

Then what's all this? I thought.

Her cat eyes narrowed into shining green sickles. "A connection, Svetlana, a special gift binding special people." She lifted an apple from a desk drawer, offering it to me. The skin of the fruit glistened, red as a deep wound. "You're a remarkable young lady, and we're going to be great friends, you and I."

Seemingly of its own accord, my hand reached for the apple.

Nine

On Saturday morning Mom called up the stairs, telling me I had visitors at the front door. It was Fumio Chen and Dwight Foote.

"Let's go to the tree house," Fumio whispered, after my mom had stepped away.

"Don't call it a tree house," I told him.

"*Whatever* you want to call it," he said.

"Don't be lame, Svet, just come on," Foote chided.

I left Razor barking in the house and followed the boys across the yard to the Oak of Doom. Foote pulled himself up the ladder using his one good arm, his bound arm bouncing in its sling. He complained the entire way and struggled to navigate through the opening in the floor.

"Get the lead out," I told him.

Fumio had already grabbed my binoculars and was

spying up Cherry Street toward Sandy's house on the corner. Over his shoulder and through the window, I saw where the trampoline used to be. The driveway was filled with unfamiliar cars. A police cruiser waited at the curb. Several men dressed in suits and uniforms stood about on the front porch.

Foote elbowed between us and began snapping photographs of the house with his digital camera.

"Did you watch the news last night?" Fumio asked.

"No," I said, pushing them aside and claiming my binoculars.

"The girls vanished into thin air," Foote said. "All three of them—just like Mr. Boyd."

"Only they didn't skip town in a souped-up Corvette with a stash of cash," Fumio mused. "Something bad happened to them."

Something bad. The words rang like a knell.

I lowered the binoculars and studied Fumio's quiet face. "Bad?"

"The news didn't say anything one way or the other," Foote noted.

"'Cause they don't know anything," Fumio said. "The next time anyone sees those girls, it's gonna be on a milk carton."

Imbeciles, I thought. They were just talking to hear themselves. "What do you two want, anyway?"

"We don't want nothing," he said.

"That means you want *something,* dork," I corrected.

"We're riding over to City Park to help out with the search—we thought you might want to go with us,"

Foote offered. "People think the girls could've gone off into the woods and gotten lost."

Fumio said, "Of course, the chances of those three prima donnas hiking off into the woods is less than zero."

"It was on the news last night that they want volunteers to show up for the search. You should come along." Foote nodded his big head, blinking his blueberry eyes.

"I can't," I said. "I've got to help my next-door neighbor today." I was supposed to go over to Lenora Bones's house at noon and read, which I was actually looking forward to—and not just because I was being paid.

"The Bone Lady, who was spying on you?"

"She's all right," I said. "She just wants someone to read to her."

Foote said, "Well, we gotta go. I'm going to take photos of the searchers at the park and Fumio's going to write up a piece for the school paper."

"But the school will never let us print it," Fumio said. "They're not going to say anything if those three girls don't show up. It's gonna be unmentionable, man."

"Totally taboo," Foote agreed.

I watched through the binoculars as a police officer left the Cross residence and climbed into the cruiser parked at the curb.

"They'll show up," I said, my gut telling me otherwise.

"Are you going to the carnival tonight?" Foote asked, meaning the Spring Fling at the school.

"It's usually pretty lame, but they'll have bumper cars," Fumio said.

"I don't know. Maybe." I lowered the binoculars. The

60

police car drove away with its emergency lights off, turning at the corner and disappearing. I wondered if it was heading to the park to join the searchers.

After the guys had left, Mom called me into the kitchen and gave me a tub of strawberry sauce and some sponge cake to take next door with me.

"Those two boys seemed nice," she said.

"They're okay."

She pushed the seal closed around the plastic container and placed it inside a grocery bag along with the cake and the empty plate from the sugar cookies we'd finished eating. "Be sure to thank Ms. Bones for those cookies."

"I will—I'm not a jerk."

When Mom smiles, her face crinkles up and tiny crow's-feet appear at the corners of her eyes. Her face crinkled now as she grabbed and squeezed me, hard enough that I almost dropped the cake.

"Whoa," I said.

"Hey, sweetie." The smile was gone from her face when she pulled away, still holding onto my shoulders. "I don't want you wandering off—okay? I want you to stick around the house this weekend and come home right after you've finished reading to Ms. Bones, do you hear?"

She was thinking about Sandy Cross and her friends.

"Dwight and Fumio asked if I wanted to go to the school carnival later," I said.

"I guess you know about those lost girls?"

"Sure," I said. "Kids at school were talking about it. I'm fine, Mom."

"Well, I'm sure those girls are fine, too. They'll probably show up later today."

"Probably," I echoed, not believing it even as I said the words. Why did I think something awful had happened to them? I'd had a bad feeling all week, since the very first day of school, really. It was almost as if there was something dangerous in the air, something inescapable. "They're just lost," I said.

Just lost.

But sometimes lost things never get found.

Ten

Lenora Bones opened her front door, and I was drowned in the delicious aroma of fresh-baked cookies. "What a beautiful smile on your face!" The old lady beamed, beckoning me to enter, her dainty fingers drawing me inside. "And exactly on time! Very good!"

She closed the door, latching little fingers onto my wrist, pulling me after her. Her frail frame was lost inside a long red dress that dusted the floor. White cuffs were fastened around her thin wrists, and a starched collar was buttoned high around her slender neck. Her silvery hair fell in curls, framing her narrow face. Gray eyes sparkled. She flashed a porcelain-white smile. "Do you smell that wonderful smell?" *Flash.*

"Yes." The sweet smell wrapped me.

"I smell it, too." Lenora Bones laughed lightly, tugging me along. "Come, Svetlana."

The house was practically devoid of furnishings. A padded straight-backed chair was the sole item in the living room. There were no shelves, no knickknacks, no pictures on the walls. Heavy black curtains were drawn closed.

"I have stacks of unpacked boxes in the den, but I can't say I'll ever bother opening them. I'm uncertain how long my stay in Sunny Hill will be," she explained.

I followed her slight figure through the house. The dining room was completely bare. In the kitchen, a square table with matching wooden chairs was pushed against the wall. A large black leather-bound book rested on the tabletop.

"But you've just moved here," I said.

She turned. "I hadn't intended to take up residence, but after finding you, I knew I had to stay a bit. That's the very reason I chose this house."

"After finding me?"

She lifted a twig-like finger to her face and tap-tapped the side of her nose. "A fortuitous discovery." She relieved me of my burden, taking the bag containing the cookie plate and the dessert my mother had prepared. "Strawberries and sponge cake, how perfect," she said without glancing inside.

"How—"

"It's all over your face, sweet girl!" She patted my cheek with the tips of her fingers. Her touch was like the delicate brushing of feathers against my skin. "You'll have to give your dear mother my thanks—if she can ever forgive me."

Forgive her? I didn't understand half of what this old lady was talking about. Could the poor woman be senile?

Lenora Bones chuckled. "Ha! Not quite! But I doubt I'll be a very good influence on you, I'm afraid, Svetlana. Or, at least, I doubt your mother will think so! Of course, she won't have to know a thing if we can help it. That would be for the best, I think."

"Won't have to know what?"

"Do you mind if we try some of this before we begin?" She pulled out the tub and the sponge cake and went to work divvying up two bowls of dessert, slicing the wedge of cake into two enormous pieces and ladling on the rich strawberry sauce until everything was completely covered. "Nice and red," she announced, glancing playfully from the brimming bowls to my smiling wonderment.

"Do you—"

"Oh, yes," the old lady crooned, spooning a mouthful of strawberries. "Mmm. I have a decided preference for the taste of red." She winked. "Let's adjourn to the back patio, shall we? I have raspberry tea already prepared."

Lenora Bones carried her dessert along, plucking the leather-bound book from the kitchen table as she passed. She slid the glass door open with a buckled boot, calling me to follow.

The patio was a half-moon shape of clay-colored flagstones shaded by the sprawling limbs of a twisted oak. A cardinal splashed in a rusted birdbath, taking wing, whistling off into the warming afternoon. There was a wrought-iron table with two padded chairs. Steam lifted from the spout of a china teapot centered on a silver tray. The old lady poured hot pink tea into delicate porcelain cups, adding a splash of milk to her own. "Do you like?" she wondered.

"Please," I answered, watching her spotted hands measuring milk into my tea. With silver tongs, I dropped two cubes of sugar into my cup. I'd never tasted hot tea before.

Ms. Bones studied me from across her cup. "I wonder, what is your favorite thing to read, Svetlana?"

I glanced to the large black volume she'd set aside on the table. I sipped the tea and thought of all the books I had ever read. Was there anything that I didn't enjoy? "I'm not sure."

"I bet you love adventure stories," she said. "And ghost stories. And science fiction." She slurped her tea and cut away a forkful of cake. "I like travel stories myself; adventures in exotic places."

I swallowed my own bite of cake, reaching for my book bag. "I brought a couple of books with me. I didn't know if you already had something in mind for us to read." I pulled out *Tarzan of the Apes* and *Treasure Island,* books I'd read before.

"Oh, those are good," she said. "But I do have a particular book for us already, a bit of nonfiction, I'm afraid. I've read it myself a number of times, but the information is terribly important, well worth revisiting. I'm hoping you'll take a special interest in it as well." She pushed the black volume across the table.

The book was as big as a box of cereal and as thick as a door. There were no markings on the cover, no title on the spine, no author's name. It smelled like a new shoe, though it was obviously old, its cover soft and worn. I opened it and found the first pages blank. The third page offered only a design at its center, a series of circles arranged into a symbol. There were three circles, two the size of a quarter, one black and one white, and a third circle no bigger than the fingernail on my pinkie, a spot as round and red as a droplet of blood. The larger circles barely touched, and where they met, the red circle was fixed. I stared at the symbol, feeling as if the larger circles were eyes peering up at me from the page.

"This is you, Svetlana," Lenora Bones said, reaching and tapping the end of her slender finger to the spot of red. "This is who *we* are." Her voice had taken on gravity, a solemnity reflected in her eyes. She looked from the page to my puzzled expression. She pressed her finger to each of the two larger circles. "The natural and the unnatural," she explained. "And in between . . . the Circle of Red." She lifted her hand from the book and gently touched my face. The sweet aroma of cookies filled my nose.

"It's you," I said. "The cookie smell is *you*."

"And you as well. Isn't it wonderful?"

Her eyes were bright with happiness, but as she continued peering into my face, the joy melted slowly from hers, dissolving into worried concern. "You're so young," she whispered, almost to herself.

The words embarrassed me somehow. I dropped my eyes back to the book, turning the page. Three words were handwritten in bold black print: *What Is Known*. The page that followed had a list of chapters and page numbers. I read down the chapter titles: *Lycanthrope, The Kraken, Zombies and Re-Animated Flesh, Sorcery (Old Country), Sorcery (Voodoo and Latin America), Water Spirits, The Tribe of Qwer-*

ril, Bloodstones and Possession. I looked up from the list into the old woman's studied gaze.

"Where I think we should begin reading," she said, "and where I think it will most benefit us to start, is Chapter Thirteen."

I moved my finger down the contents page to Chapter Thirteen, the chapter titled *Vampyres and the Corruption of Blood*. As I took in the words, a strange constriction wrapped my chest, pressing over my heart.

Does the subject interest you, Svetlana?

The whisper came into my mind, but not shockingly so. The old woman smiled slyly, pouring herself another cup of tea. She motioned toward my half-empty cup, and I shook my head no, eyeing her carefully. She set the teapot aside.

You do not seem surprised. She sent the thought to me as she sipped her tea. *That's very good.* Her words played inside my mind like smoky tendrils, uncoiling behind my eyes and tickling the inside of my skull.

She's another one, I thought. *The same as me, the same as Ms. Larch.*

Across the table the old woman suddenly faltered, the blood draining from her face. She dropped the china cup. It slipped from her fingers and shattered on the flagstones. A wave of panic, not completely my own, washed through my mind. Ms. Bones reached across the tabletop and clutched my hand, her bony fingers squeezing.

I winced. "Ouch."

Who? She asked loudly—*thought* loudly—her voice lifting inside my head like a pressurized wave, filling my mind completely. It pushed against my skull with the force of hot air expanding inside a balloon. I grimaced and pulled free of her grasp.

"Who?" she demanded. The question croaked from her trembling lips this time. She moved around the table and laid spidery hands on my shoulders. She was barely as tall as I was. Her slate-gray eyes searched my face. "You've seen her?"

"Seen who?" I asked.

"Her! She's—she's shared your thoughts?"

"Ms. Larch?"

Lenora Bones whispered the name, tasting the sound of it: "Ms. Larch." She reached her hands to my face, palms cool against my cheeks. I was smothered in the warm bakery smell. *Ms. Larch,* she thought, not in my mind this time but within her own, where I found it. She returned slowly to her seat, the hard bottoms of her black boots crackling over broken china. She paid no notice. The liveliness that had painted her face before was gone completely now, replaced with worried dread. "You know her?"

She's one of my teachers at school, I thought, forming the words inside the old woman's mind.

Lenora Bones fixed me with an appraising look, approving, smiling a mirthless grin. *And you've spoken to her? Like this?*

Yes.

She brooded, staring below the wrought-iron table at the points of the polished boots poking from beneath her red dress. She kneaded her brow, working the pads of bony fingers in circles across her wrinkled forehead, as if to conjure a thought. Finally, she cocked an eyebrow and asked, "Did she ever touch you?"

"Touch me?"

"Grab you? Try to take you?"

"Take me? Where?"

"Away. . . . Believe me, she has plans for you, my dear. I think it's only your ignorance that's saved you."

Ignorance? Who did this old lady think she was talking to? I'm no Einstein, but I'm not chopped liver, either.

Lenora Bones chuckled. "I don't mean 'ignorant' in a critical fashion, sweet girl. I only surmise that your lack of understanding in this matter has spared you thus far."

Could she read my every thought?

Not every thought—and none at all, if that's your wish. Only an unguarded thought can be read.

"You're not helping with my lack of understanding," I said, tired of talking in circles.

"No—you're quite right. And I apologize. You're extremely lucky. I should have contacted you sooner, but I had no idea she was masquerading as a teacher at your school. She's diabolical, indeed."

I reached into my book bag and pulled out the folded copy of the *Sunny Hill Bee* that Fumio Chen had given me earlier in the week. I opened it to page three and handed it to Ms. Bones. "That's her: Ms. Larch."

Lenora Bones studied the photo Dwight Foote had taken of Sylvia Larch standing in front of the school. Her wrinkled face crinkled into a hard mask of recognition. I couldn't read her thoughts, but her anger was evident, falling away in waves of primal heat. The force of her emotion unsettled me.

"I'm sorry," she said, sensing my discomfort. Her face relaxed. Her anger, as palpable as the heat from a boiling pot, faded.

"Do you know her?" I asked.

"I know *of* her. But in England she was Diana Frost, a nurse at Kensington Hospital."

"A nurse?"

"Not one you'd want to have looking after you," she said, shaking her head. "How did Larch approach you?"

"On my first day of school—she knew."

"Knew?"

"About the red foods. That I eat only things that are red, that I sleep under the bed."

"That you what?"

"Sleep under the bed—although she said that she didn't."

"Well, who would? Unless the mattress was simply dreadful. I don't know why you would want to sleep beneath your bed, my dear."

"It's better."

Lenora Bones shrugged, lifting the knobby peaks of her sharp shoulders, and rolled her eyes. I didn't latch onto her thought, but if I had, it would probably have been something to the effect of *Whatever floats your boat.*

I said, "On my first day, Ms. Larch gave out chocolates at the end of class—she knew I wouldn't want one."

"Did she?"

"She kept me after class. . . . She tried to give me an apple."

71

The old woman cocked an eyebrow. "And you took it?"

"No, I ran. I was scared."

"Of course."

"But yesterday . . ." I reached to the bottom of my book bag and found the apple Ms. Larch had given me after class on Friday. I'd forgotten all about it. I had taken it from her in a daze. Her words came back to me: *We're going to be great friends, you and I.* The fruit was bruised now, splotches of ugly brown forming on the dying skin.

Lenora Bones eyed the apple coolly, reaching and taking it cautiously from my hand. "And what else?"

"She said that she knew who I was."

"Did she?"

"I asked if . . ."

You asked her if you were a vampire? Lenora Bones thought, her face registering surprise.

"Yes."

The old woman's lips curled upward at the corners of her mouth, but the smile never reached her eyes. *I'm sorry,* she thought, *I really should have moved with greater urgency after finding you.* She reached and lifted the hem of her dress over the top of her black boot. The boot extended slightly above her ankle and was cinched with five silver buckles. Her pale shin, barely the thickness of the slender end of a baseball bat, disappeared into the boot top. A silver knife handle was tucked into the leather. *It's only that . . . I've never encountered an Olfactive so young. I'd hoped to discuss this with the others.* She pulled the stiletto from her boot. Five inches of pointed steel gripped in a tiny fist.

"The others?"

"The Circle of Red." Lenora Bones deftly divided the apple in two, tossing the pieces onto the grass beyond the rusted birdbath. A cardinal dropped from the oak, hopping toward the fruit, cocking its head, eyeing us with caution as it darted its beak into the bruised offering.

The Circle of Red, I thought, turning my attention to the open book and its bizarre list of chapters: Chapter Seventeen—*Recognizing Shape-Shifters,* Chapter Twenty-two—*Modern Ghouls.* I thumbed through the pages, crammed with blocky handwriting. Some of the writing was terribly small, barely discernible. Other pages offered crude maps. There were pages spotted with smears of ink, notes in the margins, oily smudges and stains that might have been ketchup—or something else. "You wrote this?"

"Some of it," she said. "I and other members of the Circle."

"And you want me to read it?"

"We should begin with Chapter Thirteen."

"Because of Ms. Larch?"

"Yes."

"Because she's a vampire?"

"Yes." The old woman narrowed her eyes.

"And we're not?"

"No," she said, softly. "We're more than that." She wiped the slender blade across her dress and slid it back into her boot. "We are the ones who know." Once again, she laid a finger to the side of her nose. "I was searching for Diana Frost—Ms. Larch—when I happened upon you. As you say, I have a pleasant odor about me—and you are equally sweet to my nose. I was riding the streets hunting for Larch when I caught your scent: a happy accident."

"Hunting?"

"To destroy the Kensington Vampire."

To destroy? I couldn't imagine this slight woman destroying anything. An aspirin, maybe.

She smiled ruefully. *No, I'm not so formidable as I once was. The Circle of Red grows smaller, and we in it grow older. We have not claimed a new member for many years—until now. I'd not expected to survive the Kensington Assignment, but perhaps with your help. . . .*

"I'm not destroying anyone," I said.

Lenora Bones nodded solemnly. "It's good that you do not wish to." She looked away from my face, her eyes urging mine to follow. My gaze fell beyond the birdbath to the divided apple, and the body of the crimson cardinal lying dead beside it, poisoned.

But it's not a choice you have, my sweet.

Eleven

According to the book *What Is Known*, anyone can become a vampire. It requires only the corruption of blood.

"Corruption?"

"Blood can become spoiled, tainted by misdeed," the old woman explained.

I had read the recommended Chapter Thirteen twice. "This is nuts," I said. "You expect me to believe this? So if I drink a frog's blood or something . . . I'll become a vampire?" That was ridiculous.

"No, dear," Ms. Bones corrected. "There's not enough blood in a frog. And only by drinking the blood of a human, can a human be corrupted. A steady diet of blood will lead to the corruption of one's own blood. A corrupted soul dies, and in dying, human feeling is lost. A vampire is born."

"And lives forever?"

"A long time, certainly," the old woman said. "Centuries, perhaps."

"That's a lot of blood."

"Yes—and many innocent victims."

I pushed my empty dessert plate away, glad I'd eaten before all this talk of blood. I put aside the leather-bound book. I was open to weird and strange—but not *this* weird and strange. Across the table, Ms. Bones watched as I collected my copies of *Tarzan of the Apes* and *Treasure Island* as well as the *Sunny Hill Bee*. I slid them back into my book bag.

"My mom's gonna be worried if I don't get home soon," I said, ready to be gone.

The old woman frowned. What did she want from me, anyhow? To help her destroy my science teacher? That wasn't going to happen. I could handle a little ESP and a steady diet of watermelon, but I wasn't going to get into any kind of life and death struggle with anyone or anything. I'd thought that maybe I was a vampire, but I was wrong. Which was all right—I could live with that. After all, I was kind of fond of my soul. According to the old woman's black book, being a vampire was a pretty lousy deal anyway. And I could just as easily live without belonging to the so-called Circle of Red, too.

I know this is asking a great deal, but it won't be a poisoned apple you're dodging next time, dear girl. And perhaps you'll not be so lucky.

The old woman's thought seeped into my head. Was this a sales pitch? Was she making puppy dog eyes at me? *Yeah? Well, it sounds like it's your job to take care of that—the Circle of Red's job, right?*

"The power this vampire knows is an addiction. Blood is the cost—and murder." Ms. Bones laid her hand over mine. "Now that Sylvia Larch is aware of what you are, she cannot let you live."

"I'm nothing." I pulled my hand away.

"You belong to the Circle, whether you like it or not—it's in your blood. You have the nose, Svetlana. You smell the rot on her. To the Kensington Vampire you are equally foul. This is not something you get to choose; it chooses you." Lenora Bones grabbed my hand once more.

I tried pulling away, but this time her grip was unbreakable.

"The Circle has been fantastically lucky in discovering the Kensington Vampire," she said. "This creature might have preyed on the blood of innocents for centuries."

I couldn't turn away from the hardness in the old woman's stare. Her fingers were like steel bands around my wrist.

"Many have suffered already. I was fortunate to rediscover the monster's trail after she escaped me in London. If I lose her here, I might never again have the chance to defeat her. Is that what you want?"

Let go. I twisted my arm, willing her to release me.

She removed her bony hand, perhaps by choice. "You must do what you can to help, Svetlana. The power is inside you."

The thought I had was this: *You might consider changing your name to the Circle of Useless.*

I was not impressed.

Twelve

So I wasn't a vampire, big deal. Had it been an unreasonable assumption? I didn't think so: eat only red, sleep under the bed, heightened sensory perception, mind control, looking fantastic in black. It had definitely been plausible.

"How did it go over there?" Mom asked when I returned home.

"Okay!" I yelled over my shoulder as I ran up the stairs. I didn't want to talk about it. What could I tell her? That Lenora Bones had tried to recruit me into an international secret society of crazy old ladies? In my room, I changed into my favorite black T-shirt and black jeans. Mom had made me dress up before going over to the Bone Lady's house. In the front yard Razor was going nuts, running in frantic circles around the bottom of the Oak of Doom, yapping his head off. I peered down from my bedroom window and wondered if Fumio Chen and

Dwight Foote had sneaked through the front gate and climbed up into my hideout. But it was barely four o'clock, so I figured they were probably still at the park, helping with the search for the missing girls.

I tried to imagine Sandy, Marsha, and Madison sleeping outside in the woods overnight. Two nights, actually—it was Saturday, and they hadn't been seen since Thursday afternoon. I decided the girls couldn't have been lost in the woods for that long, not anywhere around Sunny Hill. It wasn't like there was some big wilderness out there to get lost in.

Fumio and Foote had said they'd come by later to see if I wanted to go with them to the Spring Fling Carnival. The soccer field at school had been fenced off yesterday so carnival workers could set up amusement rides and booths. It might be fun to go. There was a good-sized Ferris wheel I wouldn't mind taking a spin on. I needed to get out and go somewhere this weekend, not just be cooped up around the house. Mom certainly wasn't going to let me go anywhere on my own—at least not until the missing girls showed up. But she'd probably let me go with Fumio and Foote. I had a couple bucks in my secret stash that I could spend, not much.

I'd hoped to make some decent cash reading to the Bone Lady, but that job had turned out to be a complete bust. I couldn't go back there. Ms. Bones's eyesight was fine. I should have suspected as much since she didn't even wear eyeglasses. I liked the old woman a lot—you can't help liking someone who smells like cookies. But I didn't see any good coming from hanging around her.

She was on the hunt for Ms. Larch. Unbelievable! And she actually wanted me to help destroy my own science teacher, whatever that meant. The science teacher was definitely a bit off, no doubt—my nose informed me of that much. But a vampire? A vampire the same as one in Lenora Bones's black book? Heck, I'd thought *I* was a vampire—and that turned out to be a mistake. Maybe the entire situation with Ms. Larch was just a crazy mix-up, too.

That's what I told myself. But what I pictured was the apple Ms. Larch had given me, the one Lenora Bones had cut into two pieces. I saw the poor cardinal lying dead on the ground, its bright red feathers gone dull in death. Had Larch really tried to poison me? When I stepped into her classroom, did she smell the stench of rotted meat coming off me—the same as I smelled from her? Was I her foe, then, whether I liked it or not? Lenora Bones said it was in my blood, that I was one of the Circle of Red, a guardian between the natural and the unnatural. She said I had no choice.

Outside, Razor continued sniffing and barking around the bottom of the giant oak.

"Svetlana!" Mom called.

I knew she wanted me to go outside and calm down Razor. Sometimes he went crazy over squirrels, or a cat that had the dumb luck to sneak over the fence. Of course, if Razor ever went toe to toe with a cat, he'd probably get the shock of his furry little life.

Razor stopped barking and rushed over when I banged through the door onto the front porch. He looked up at me as if to say: What took you so long? His little ears were lifted, and his stinger tail poked up straight as an antenna. He led me to the Oak of Doom, and I climbed up the ladder, but there was no one inside the hideout. I did a double take at the leather-bound book resting on the crate I used for a table. A torn sheet of newspaper poked from between its pages. It was the front page of today's *Sunny Hill Tribune.* The headline read: "Search Organized for Missing Girls." Above the headline, Ms. Bones had scrawled in black ink: *There's no time to waste!*

How had the Bone Lady gotten in and out of my hideout so fast? There was more to that old woman than met the eye, even beyond the fact that she kept a knife in her boot. Ms. Bones obviously believed that the three girls had run afoul of the so-called Kensington Vampire. Now that she knew Ms. Larch was the woman she sought and that she was a teacher at Sunny Hill Middle School, Lenora Bones had connected the missing girls to her. But could it be true?

I shivered, remembering the science teacher's icy touch, her red-nailed fingers cold against my cheek as she reached across her desk and whispered my name. The memory brought with it the smell of rot, the ripe odor of bad fruit and spoiled meat, the smell of garbage on a hot day when a trash can has been left sitting in the sun. I saw again the sightless eye of the dead cardinal, as black and hard as a button. I imagined Ms. Larch as a nurse, wheeling sleeping patients down a long corridor to a darkened room and their doom. The image came frighteningly easy. I could almost smell the hospital antiseptic and hear the ghostly squeaking of wheels and the *tap-tap-tapping* of stiletto heels across a cold tile floor.

"Svetlana!"

I jerked from my dark dreaming. In the street, Fumio Chen and Dwight Foote had pulled up on their bikes and were shouting at me.

"Any luck with the search?" I asked, knowing the answer already.

"Nah," Foote said. "You coming with us to the carnival or what?"

I decided a diversion would do me good. I climbed down and went inside to ask Mom. She said I could go as long as I was back home by dark, which was still a few hours away. My money wouldn't last that long, anyhow, even with the extra five bucks she gave me.

I definitely needed to get away from the black thoughts creeping around in my head.

Thirteen

On the ride over to the Spring Fling Carnival, we pedaled past telephone poles plastered with notices for the missing girls. The stapled sheets fluttered in the afternoon breeze, rustling like dry leaves. The sound made me think of fall, although it was definitely springtime. The sun was stuck in the sky like a fried egg in a pan. Before the carnival even came into sight, I could smell popcorn and fried dough. Festive music piped over the milling crowds and rows of brightly colored tents. The parking lot was jammed with cars, and more vehicles overflowed onto the grass and along the curbsides surrounding the soccer field. The bike rack was full, so we chained our bikes to a railing near the school entrance.

"This place is packed!" Fumio said, pushing his padlock closed. "Let's check out the bumper cars first, okay?"

I didn't care. The Ferris wheel rose on the far side of

the carnival, half-filled with riders against the blue sky. A banner over the soccer field entrance read: SUNNY HILL SPRING FLING CARNIVAL AND FUND-RAISER. We waited in a long line to get onto the bumper-car ride. When we finally did, it was totally lame. The junky cars crawled as slow as molasses. Unbelievably, one of the rules was to *not* bump into the other cars. The ride cost three tickets and seemed as if it was over as soon as it began, which was no big loss.

"What a freaking rip-off," Fumio complained.

"I get to choose next," Foote said.

We wandered down the rows of booths, jostling through the crowd. There were more adults at the carnival than kids. Foote and Fumio knew most of the kids, and even I knew a few. I waved to freckled Alison Finch from my gym class with her parents in tow, equally freckled. She waved back. Coach Cooper was there, sitting behind a table, trying to coax students into signing up for summer soccer league. Good luck. Her whistle dangled from a cord around her bull neck—which was hardly a neck at all. She probably wore the whistle when she went to bed at night.

"Come on, Svetlana," she called, waving me over. I acted like I didn't hear. I didn't know what I was going to do this summer, but it sure wasn't going to be running around and sweating for Coach Cooper.

Fumio wanted to stop and give the Coin Toss Challenge a try. It was a table arrayed with every imaginable shape and size of glass container: ashtrays, jelly jars, fishbowls, and so forth. The object of the game was to stand behind a rope and toss a quarter so that it landed in a jar or dish without popping out.

"And what do you win if you do it?" Foote asked.

Fumio pointed to the rows of clear plastic bags hanging from clothespins around the top of the booth. Each had a lonely goldfish swimming in it. "A goldfish, man," he said, pointing, looking exactly like the dweeb he was.

"What do you want a stupid goldfish for?" Foote asked. I wondered the same thing. Once again, Foote was looking more like the brains of the duo.

We carried on past the merry-go-round, where bored moms and dads balanced little kids on the saddles of plastic horses. We paused at the Spinning Teacup, but I nixed that idea. Forking over three tickets for the thrill of losing my lunch seemed like a bad trade. The Ferris wheel was reloading, but Foote kept us moving forward.

"What the heck?" I said.

"I'm looking for the pop guns, man. That's my game."

We went by the Jellybean Jar Count, where a ticket earned you the chance to guess the number of beans and win a brand-new baseball glove. Another booth sported a lazy-looking chicken locked inside a glass case. The chicken did math. Honestly, it was the cruelest thing I'd ever seen. Why in the world would anybody force a chicken to do math? Why was this allowed? And why would anyone want to pay to watch a chicken count corn, anyway? In the next booth over, Principal Talbot had volunteered to sit in the Dunking Tank. Two tickets got you three chances to peg a button with a tennis ball and drop the principal into a water-filled tub.

We passed by it all.

"C'mon, Foote," Fumio demanded, wanting to do *something.*

"It's right ahead," Foote said, pointing to the shooting gallery. A table lined with pop pistols fronted the booth. Tin targets shaped like little buffalo moved in mechanical circles ten feet beyond the table. It didn't seem a very far distance to shoot. The gallery was called Deadeye Shoot-'em-up.

"How much?" Foote asked, pulling tickets from his jean pocket with his good arm.

The grizzled guy behind the table had a gut that fell over his pants like a sack of water. "Two tickets, ten shots," he said, uninterestedly, scratching at his whiskered neck and gnawing on a giant pretzel he'd gotten from the booth next door.

Foote handed over a pair of tickets and hefted a pistol from the table. It looked like something a gunslinger would carry in a Wild West movie. The pistol was connected to the table by a thin hose snaking from the pearly handle; it was an air gun. Foote carefully took aim at the rotating buffalo targets and squeezed the trigger. The gun made a *Phhooot!* sound, but the buffalo ratcheted along, unfazed.

Phhooot!

Phhooot!

Phhooot!

Still nothing. "Hey, this thing isn't working right," Foote complained, holding the gun out to the booth attendant.

"Yeah, it's probably the pistol," the guy said, his sarcasm pushing through a mouthful of pretzel. He let Foote take his remaining six shots using a different air gun, but the buffalo remained unscathed.

"Dang," Foote said, frustrated.

"Do two more tickets," Fumio told him.

"Nah, I only got four left. This thing's rigged. I need both hands anyway." He wiggled the fingers poking from the cast on his left arm.

"But you're right-handed," Fumio noted.

"I need both hands to shoot steady."

Whatever. I tore off two tickets and picked up a pistol. The gun was heavier than I thought it would be.

"Ten shots for the little princess," Pretzel Guy said, tossing my tickets into a bucket.

Princess? What I wanted to do was shoot that pretzel out of his hand. Instead, I stiffened my arm and stared down the black barrel, lining the sights up along the top of the air pistol and bringing the blurry buffalo into focus.

Phhooot! The tin cutout fell over with a metal clacking sound.

Phhooot! Clack!
Phhooot! Clack!
Phhooot! Clack!

"Oh, no!" Fumio laughed, swatting Foote on his left shoulder, making him wince. "You're being totally smoked, dude!"

I paid no mind. My arm had turned to rigid steel. I listened for the barely discernible *tick-tick-ticking* of gears as the tiny buffalo cutouts circled and sprang into view. I felt the weight of displaced air as the pistol puffed. The pistol and the air were almost an extension of myself, as if I were reaching an invisible hand across the distance and knocking over the tin targets with a flick of my finger.

Phhooot! Clack!

Phhooot! Clack!

I reeled off nine shots and dropped nine buffalo.

"Whoa!" Pretzel Guy pronounced, his half-eaten twist of dough forgotten. "I've never seen anyone knock over nine in a row—impressive."

"One more and you win the grand prize!" Foote shouted, clapping my back. He pointed to a skateboard hanging from a bar above the revolving buffalo. It was a deluxe board, done up in midnight black with twin lightning bolts and premium trucks and wheels.

"C'mon, just one more, Svet," Fumio whispered.

I leveled the pistol and stared down the gun sights, bringing the buffalo into line. I released my breath and closed one eye, settling on the next target. In my mind, it was a done deal. I tickled the trigger with the end of my finger, squeezing. A shiver rippled across my scalp and down my spine. Tiny hairs along the top of my neck tingled as a ripe rotting odor filled the air. I let up on the trigger, dropping my eyes to the alabaster hand with red nails reaching across the tabletop, taking hold of the air pistol alongside my own. I looked up into the smiling face of Sylvia Larch.

"Let's see what you've got, Svetlana," she purred, her grin breaking open like a snowy chasm.

"You shoulda seen it, Ms. Larch," Fumio raved. "Svetlana just mowed through nine targets. *Bam! Bam! Bam!* One more and she's got the skateboard!"

Our teacher's eyes brimmed with amusement. Green flames danced behind her stare. I turned back to the tin targets, but they appeared farther away now. The pistol seemed heavier. I matched up the sights, but the gun barrel trembled in my grip.

"Do your best, Stephanie Grimm," Larch challenged.

I tugged the trigger and the gun spit.

Phhooot!

Nothing.

"Aarghhh," Fumio groaned.

"Oh, man!" Foote shouted.

"That's too bad," Ms. Larch breathed, her sick cherry breath rolling out rotten sweet. She lifted the air pistol in her hand and fired off nine quick shots, nine rapid pulls of the trigger. The targets fell in tumbling succession, toppling like dominoes, clacking one right after the next.

Foote whistled in awe.

"Dang, Ms. Larch," Fumio breathed, staring up at her in amazement, as if she were a goddess.

"Holy cow, lady," Pretzel Guy drooled.

Cow, I thought.

Ms. Larch cocked her elbow and swiveled to face me. She held the air pistol up, her grin flashing supermodel white. She looked spectacular in her skintight black jumpsuit with a wide bone-colored belt cinched tight around her hourglass-shaped center. She could have been an assassin from a cool spy flick.

I felt like cold oatmeal: no milk, no sugar, no cinnamon. Plain with a capital P.

Ms. Larch bit down hard on the cherry lozenge clicking between her perfect teeth. It cracked like bone. She laid down the pistol.

"Whoa! You got one more shot, Ms. Larch!" Foote said.

"You can win the game!" Fumio shouted.

She threw the boys a bored glance, dismissing them with a bat of her green eyes. Her focus fell on me. I felt like a worm popped out of the ground with a robin peeking over it.

"I don't play games," she said softly.

"Hey, that's two tickets you owe me, lady," the gallery keeper reminded her, suddenly rediscovering his pretzel and guiding it to his mouth.

Ms. Larch paid him no mind. She reached a hand to my burning cheek, and I jerked away.

Don't touch me, I thought.

I'm surprised to see you out and about, sweet Svetlana. Her oily voice seeped into my mind. *I dreamed you had a tummy ache.*

I shuddered but tried not to show it. *Dream on,* I thought.

She threw back her head and laughed aloud. Fumio and Foote exchanged confused looks.

"Hey, lady," Pretzel Guy started again, but Larch was already moving away, giving us her backside as she sashayed off into the carnival crowd. The din of music, laughter, ringing, dinging, and voices came over me in a flood, as if a pair of earmuffs had been suddenly snatched from my head.

"Dang, she can sure shoot," Fumio said. He stared after Larch's disappearing figure, his face all dreamy and pathetic.

I fought the urge to reach out and thump him one.

"Hey, you can shoot, too," Foote said, giving me a friendly punch on the shoulder.

I felt out of it, rattled by Ms. Larch and her sudden coming and going. I wrinkled my nose over her lingering stench. Her words echoed: *I dreamed you had a tummy ache.* The image of the stricken cardinal filled my head, its once bright feathers turned dull in death. Larch *had* tried to poison me, I had no doubt now. The Bone Lady was right. Could she be right about our teacher's connection to the missing girls, too?

"It's your pick this time," Fumio told me.

But I was far from a carnival mood now.

"C'mon, we've still got tickets left," Foote insisted. "You said you wanted to ride the Ferris wheel, didn't you?" He grabbed my elbow to tug me along.

"Hey," Pretzel Guy called, and I turned around. "You knocked over more than five targets, princess—you won." He grinned, reaching out my prize. I sighed and took the plastic bag with the stupid goldfish in it.

Fourteen

Fumio went off to play the coin toss, and Foote practically dragged me over to the Ferris wheel. "Snap out of it, Svet."

He'd see me snap if he called me "Svet" one more time.

The bag of water in my hand slopped from side to side, the poor goldfish wiggling to make sense of the world. At the Ferris wheel, we queued up in a short line. The giant ring of steel spokes and buckets rotated lazily to the piping of canned music.

Foote pushed his sliding-down eyeglasses back up his long nose. "You don't like Ms. Larch much, do you?"

"Why do you say that?"

"I can tell."

His magnified eyes blinked blue. His teeth were straight, except for an errant one at the bottom that leaned away from the rest like a lazy fence picket. He had a goofy look on his face—maybe a guilty look.

"What?"

"Nothing," he said, glancing away.

What was he acting all weird about?

The Ferris wheel began pausing in brief jerks as riders were let off and new ones let on. The line moved, and we handed over our tickets and dropped into a rocking bucket seat. The earth fell away as we were lifted into the air. I was taken by an uneasy sense of vertigo and gripped the safety bar. The sickly sweet odor of rot and corruption followed me, even as we moved higher into the clear sky. I had Larch on the brain.

"Well, how was your first week of school, Svet? Did you like it? You never went to a real school before, huh?"

"No."

"No to the second or the third?"

"No to three. Number one and two are okay. And don't call me Svet."

"You'll like it more—you'll see." Foote smiled sheepishly, rocking his big head.

From the top of the wheel, I could see over the roof of the school and the tops of tents and the cars parked up and down the parking lot and streets. I saw beyond the trees and roofs of nearby houses. Some of the taller downtown buildings poked up in the distance. Forested hills spread away to the east. The Ferris wheel peaked, and then we seemed to gather speed as we rotated back toward earth.

"What do you think happened to Sandy Cross and the others?" The question popped out of my mouth on its own, even though I didn't want to ask it.

Foote said he didn't know, the smile dropping away from his face. "They must be lost on the other side of City Park. It borders the national forest. They could have gotten turned around in there. I've been camping back in those woods, and anyone could lose their way, easy."

"For days?" It didn't make any sense. "They're all marked trails. And what about the girls' bikes? Searchers would have at least found their bikes if the girls had walked off into the woods."

"Maybe the bikes have been found," he said. "Mobs of searchers showed up at City Park. There was even a television news crew there. Those girls'll get found and probably end up being famous—go on *The Oprah Winfrey Show* and all that junk. Talk about how they had to eat bugs and sleep inside a rotted tree trunk to stay warm."

I liked the idea of Sandy Cross and her lame posse having to eat bugs, but I didn't think the girls had it that good. In fact, I was sure they had it much worse. I was certain the girls had fallen into the clutches of Sylvia Larch, a.k.a. Diana Frost—the Kensington Vampire. The Bone Lady was right. I didn't want to believe it, but I did. In my blood and bones, I knew it. Our creepy science teacher had freaked me out from day one. I was different—that was a fact—and Ms. Larch was different, too, but in a bad way. The nose knows, and mine knew better than most.

"Do you believe in monsters?" I asked Foote.

The wheel was launching us back into the sky. Foote

studied me with his wide face, seeing that I was serious. I appreciated that he at least considered the question.

"Do you mean like Bigfoot?"

"Maybe," I said. "Like things people don't know about—or don't talk about. I believe the missing girls have run into bad trouble, and not the kind where you get turned around in the woods. And I think Ms. Larch has something to do with it." I wanted to see his face when I said the last part, but he was looking down at the view falling away beneath us.

He eventually looked up, shaking his head. "You really don't like her at all."

"There's something wrong about Ms. Larch. I can't explain it, but I know it. I knew it the moment I stepped into her classroom." I didn't want to go overboard, but the words came spilling out. "She's just strange. The way she looks and acts. The way she dresses. It's like she's some kind of alien fashion model."

"Hey, you don't have to lose a beauty contest to be a science teacher. I like looking at Ms. Larch a lot more than I ever liked looking at Mr. Boyd—although he was definitely funnier."

Boys are so limited.

"Have you noticed how every one of her classes is about some kind of animal getting eaten by another animal, or about rats or worms or something gross?"

"You've only had her for a week—"

"And didn't you think it was weird the way she knocked over all those targets at the shooting gallery? Without hardly looking?"

95

"You did just as well as she did," he said.

But I hadn't. And I wasn't exactly normal myself.

"Just 'cause she's good looking doesn't make her a monster," he went on. "And I don't think you're a monster, either."

What was he talking about? He glanced away shyly, then quickly turned back. What was that dumb look on his face? Suddenly, he was reaching in with puckered lips to kiss me. I pulled away, but not before he bumped his big head into mine. What the heck! Without thinking, I drew back and punched him hard on his right shoulder. He yelped and reached with his bandaged left arm, yelping again as he moved his cast too quickly.

"You do that again and I'll break your good arm," I huffed, feeling the hot flush of blood on my cheeks. *Jerk*. I lifted the goldfish bag and apologized to the little fish for sloshing its water. The poor creature didn't have a clue. It popped into my head then to name the fish "Dwight."

"Hey, I think you're cool, that's all," he stammered, his face as red as mine felt.

What was going on in that bonehead's thick skull? I said, "Don't read too much into this Ferris wheel ride, Foote. This isn't a date."

Just then the wheel began a jerking descent as riders below were expelled. Our bucket seat rocked back and forth in the fading sunlight.

"I think I need to go home now," I said. "My mom's gonna blame me for every gray hair on her head if I don't get back before dark."

"I'll go find Fumio," he said, looking away.

When we reached the bottom, we jumped from the bucket and rejoined the carnival mob on the ground. I went toward where we'd chained our bikes, kicking myself for having said anything at all to Foote about Ms. Larch. There was nothing gained in that. I needed to talk to Lenora Bones and find out what she had in mind. The old lady was right—I didn't have a choice in any of this. I could see that now.

I unchained my bike from the railing and pushed it to the sidewalk, holding the swinging goldfish bag against the handlebar. Mom would probably think the fish was a bad idea, but what could I do? Calliope music piped over the coming evening. Floodlights began snapping on around the carnival and school grounds. The parking lot was still jam-packed with vehicles.

I waited curbside for Fumio and Foote, wondering at how crazy the world had become this week. But really, everything had been cartwheeling toward crazy for some time now. For months I'd felt different, acted different. Lenora Bones said I was special. Even Ms. Larch said I was special—but she said so in the most menacing way. One thing was for sure: I needed to get a grip. The world had become a very dangerous place. Sandy, Marsha, and Madison were history, and if I didn't watch out, I was next.

"Watch out!"

Foote's warning cry turned my head just as the squeal of tires filled my ears. A white van swerved, crashing over the curb onto the sidewalk. The unseen driver steered directly toward where I stood holding my bicycle. There was no doubt of the driver's deadly intention.

The van blotted my vision, barreling down on me like an unstoppable locomotive. The world froze into halting frames, became a movie reel slowed to a jerking crawl. I saw clouds and sky reflected in the widening windshield. The approaching headlights became cold eyes; the front grill, a silver rack of menacing teeth. The engine growled hungrily, the sound expanding into a deafening roar as the van rocketed toward me.

I buckled my legs and then launched, my knees uncoiling like springs as I hurtled myself backward over my bicycle. I was airborne. There was a loud smack as the van caught the edge of the handlebar, jerking the bike away and sending it clattering down the sidewalk. The van's side mirror swished by, a hair's breadth from my face. I fell back and tumbled onto my butt and elbows, rolling away in the grass. The van thumped over the curb and dropped back onto the street, tires squealing as it sped away.

Foote and Fumio were instantly on either side of me, dragging me to my feet.

"Holy guacamole!" Fumio shouted.

What was he yelling about? I was the one who'd almost been flattened into a tortilla.

I rubbed at my elbow where the skin was scraped and bleeding.

"Are you okay?" Foote asked, looking me up and down.

"You were so dead!" Fumio continued in a loud voice, shouting into my ear.

"Geez . . ." I pushed him away. I scratched at the back of my head where I'd banged it, luckily on the grass and not the sidewalk. "I think I'm okay." I dabbed at the blood on my elbow.

"That was amazing! That was . . . completely amazing! You should be total roadkill, man." Fumio's excitement bordered on happiness.

"That was close," Foote said, staring down the street where the van had disappeared.

"It was her," I breathed.

"Don't be nuts."

"Her?" Fumio said.

"Larch—Ms. Larch. She wants me dead."

"Do you know how crazy that sounds?" Foote said, real concern in his voice.

Fumio's face was a mask of confusion. "Our science teacher?"

My body began to tremble now that the danger had passed, at least for the moment. But Fumio was right; I *had* almost been roadkill. "It was Ms. Larch," I said, and I was sure of it. The two boys stared. "She tried to poison me before. And now this. She's got Sandy Cross and her friends, and she knows that I know it."

"You must've really whacked your head," Fumio said.

"Let's go find the nurse and tell somebody," Foote suggested, putting his hand gently on my shoulder.

I shrugged it off. "Forget it—you're not listening to me."

"Are you listening to yourself?" Fumio said. "You sound like a nut job. That was some drunk driver—or someone on a cell phone driving like an idiot. Nobody's trying to kill you, Svetlana. Get over yourself."

"Did you see that it was her driving?" Foote asked.

"It was her." I had no doubt. "You know what I said on the Ferris wheel, about monsters? She's one—a vampire. A killer."

Foote looked embarrassed for me.

Fumio let out a long whistle. "I think you've suffered a psychic break, kiddo." He said it trying to be funny, but it wasn't.

I walked over to where my bike had landed and righted it. The rubber grip on the handlebar was shredded and the mirror was bent and shattered. Seven years bad luck for someone. But otherwise the bike seemed intact. The sun was a dying coal on the horizon. Orange streaks lengthened across the sky. I had to get home. "It doesn't matter if you believe me or not," I said, almost in a whisper. "But you'd better watch yourself around her."

Fumio shook his head. "'Cause she's a monster?"

Down the street, a black sports car growled out of the school parking lot. The car eased up the road, coming to a stop alongside us. The engine purred. It was a convertible with the top up. The windows were tinted dark, the driver invisible. We stood watching and waiting, reflected in the black glass—three kids huddled around a bicycle.

The passenger window glided down with an electronic whirring, and a beautiful face leaned out from the shadows, green eyes glinting. I felt my heart squeezed, as if an invisible hand had reached inside my chest. "Are you kids all right?" Ms. Larch asked. Her face seemed to glow, floating like a mask.

"Yes, ma'am," Fumio said, shaking his head and looking at me.

The science teacher's smile flashed in the darkness, and then was lost as the tinted window whirred closed. The sleek car glided away like a shark.

We watched it turn at the corner and disappear. No one said a word until Foote said, "I'm sorry, Svetlana."

He was staring down at the grass. I followed his gaze and found the clear plastic bag broken open and empty. The goldfish lay on its side, as still and lifeless as the poisoned redbird.

Fifteen

That night I tried sleeping on top of the bed, but it was unbearable. The mattress was comfortable enough, but I felt completely exposed. The ceiling seemed so far away. After tossing and turning for nearly an hour, I grabbed my blanket and pillow and crawled beneath the box spring. I needed the closeness all around me, the firm reassurance of the hard floor beneath the folds of my comforter. I curled up in the darkness with a flashlight and a Sherlock Holmes adventure, reading until I finally fell asleep.

I was awakened by a half-heard whisper. Had someone called my name? The book was still in my hands, the flashlight still on. I clicked it off. I scooted out from beneath the bed and sat cross-legged on the floor, listening. Moonlight fell through the window, casting a rectangle of milky brightness across the floor.

Svetlana . . .

The whisper was not in my ears but in my head.

Svetlana . . .

I crawled on my hands and knees and knelt at the windowsill, peeking down onto the front yard. There was a soft glow coming from inside the tree house.

Svetlana . . .

The plastic rooster on the dresser was also a clock; the hands across its belly showed 3:11. I slipped a flannel shirt over my pajama top and crept quietly from my bedroom. Dad's faint snoring came through the closed door across the hallway. I heard his heart beating, and my mother's heart, too, softer and slower. They were both sound asleep. I crept down the stairs, carefully skipping the seventh and twelfth steps, the ones that squeaked loudest. The refrigerator hummed. The clock on the kitchen wall ticked. Razor looked up from his sleeping pad on the floor. I lifted my finger to my lips and breathed, "Shh." He rested his head back on his crossed paws, his eyes shining in the darkness. I tiptoed through shadows to the front door, and then outside onto the moonlit porch. Leaves whispered in the trees.

Svetlana . . .

All right, all right, I thought.

I crossed the yard. Stiff grass tickled the bottoms of my bare feet. I climbed the wooden slats up the Oak of Doom and into the hideout. The room was thick with the smell of warm cookies. The Bone Lady was seated in the lone chair before the makeshift table, her eyes closed. She paid me no mind as I poked my head through the opening in the floor and pulled myself up into the tiny space, taking a seat on the floor against the wall. I pulled my flannel shirt closed against the night chill. The old woman had a dark housecoat wrapped tight around her knobby shoulders. A candle glowed on the tabletop, the naked flame shivering.

Lenora Bones opened her eyes and found me. She lifted the torn newspaper clipping from her black book—the article concerning the three missing girls.

Do you know these young ladies?

They're in some of my classes.

In Ms. Larch's class?

Yes.

Her face appeared unnaturally gaunt and pale in the dim light. Her cheeks were sunken, and wrinkles crisscrossed her skin like fine cracks in a china cup. She smiled, but sadly.

I said before and I say again: You are very young, dear girl. I was well into my nineteenth year before the change came to me—and I was young for it myself, though soon old enough to be a grieving widow.

Her face had the character of stone. Her eyes, twin gray pebbles, reflected the candlelight. The old woman's thoughts took shape in my mind like thickening smoke.

My lovely David, my husband of barely a year, lost his life to the indiscriminate evil of a black-hearted ghoul. That was how I first came to know of the Circle of Red—and it of me. David served as a police detective, you see. He and his men had no idea of the evil they were battling. I later destroyed the ghoul myself, working with Daphne St. Simone, perhaps the greatest Olfactive ever to wear the Red.

She opened the neck of her housecoat to display a crimson stone—red, but almost black in the candlelight. It dangled from a silver chain about her throat. The chain was thin; the stone, flat and the size of a thumbnail.

An Olfactive? I thought.

Lenora Bones tapped the side of her nose. *Just as we are.*

But what are *we?*

We are the ones who know—when no one else knows. We feel it, we see it, smell it, taste it in the very air. Our senses are heightened, attuned to the rhythms of the natural world. We are sensitive to the grotesque and the aberrant.

I didn't know what to think and finally just said, "Wow." The old woman remained motionless, studying me. I thought, *Okay, so there's this group, with people like me, who . . .*

Why do we eat only red? I asked—thought.

Well, you can eat anything you like, but red simply tastes better.

Which was true.

My legs were growing stiff from sitting on the floor, and I climbed to my feet. The wood floor was cold, and it creaked as I paced to and fro. Outside, crickets chirped in the moonlight. *But what do we do? You say . . . you say you work for the Circle of Red?*

I wouldn't say I work *for the Circle. That's just who we are, dear. We're . . . kind of a club, really.*

But you were assigned to destroy the Kensington Vampire?

Yes. But not like a job assignment. It's like . . . a calling, really. It's as if a person had wings, they'd have to fly, wouldn't they?

Hmm . . . I guess. I just couldn't see the upside to any of this. "Well," I started but then thought: *What good is it? I mean—sensitive to the grotesque and the aberrant? Who wants that?*

Lenora Bones burst out laughing, and I found myself standing with my hands on my hips, waiting for her to stop, which she did, finally, still shaking her head and grinning. "Svetlana, when you view it like that, I guess there is no upside—other than being able to help those in need. Because of your gift—which you can argue is no gift at all—you have a responsibility. A duty to protect the innocent."

"To fight evil?"

"Well . . ." The old woman didn't say anything more. I could almost see the wheels turning inside her head, feel her thoughts forming. I understood, even without the words.

"So how do we stop the Kensington Vampire?" I asked.

Lenora Bones reached for my hand, held it between her ten delicate fingers. "Poor, poor girl," she said, kissing my knuckles, pressing her lips gently to the back of my fingers. "I wish we didn't have to act, but we do, and soon. We must move quickly to save the missing girls."

"Then Sandy and her friends are still alive?"

"Perhaps," she said. "A vampire must have a constant supply of fresh blood, but only a pint a day is required. If possible, they keep their victims alive for days or even weeks, slowly draining them of their life force."

For some reason, I pictured a demented dairy farm. Which was totally gross. "You mean like milking a cow?"

"Well . . . not exactly. I wouldn't say like a cow. But . . . yes—kind of like that, I suppose."

"But how can we stop her?"

Lenora Bones opened her black book, flipping through to Chapter Thirteen: *Vampyres and the Corruption of Blood*. She ran a bony finger down the page. "A dart tipped with juice from the kalanga berry is ideal, but that's seasonal and found primarily in Madagascar. . . ." She flipped the page. "Decapitation, of course; removal of the heart or stake through the heart; salt water—if the vampire can be submerged for more than two hours, that is. Um . . ." She turned to the next page. "Burning . . . Also, there was a case in Spain where a vampire was destroyed with a laser—"

"Okay," I interrupted, not seeing the point to any of those suggestions. "Forget about kalanga berries and lasers—they're out. If we were near the ocean, maybe the saltwater option, but . . ." It didn't seem likely. "And I have to tell you," I said, "I'm not excited about the decapitation or heart thing." Which was a colossal understatement. The old lady definitely had some wild ideas.

"There's no pretty way to do this, Svetlana."

"But why not just call the police?"

"And tell them what? That we can direct them to the Kensington Vampire?" Lenora Bones shook her head. "At best we might save the girls, but Diana Frost would almost certainly escape, and many innocent victims would suffer in the future. The police are unable to comprehend the danger of such a creature, believe me. She must be stopped *forever.*"

"Well, how do you usually do it?" I asked.

Lenora Bones blinked, and then shrugged. She crossed her arms and fell into quiet thought. After a moment, her shoulders slumped. "To be honest, Sister Marguerite generally handles the vampires."

"You're saying you've never done this before?"

Well, no—not this. Technically no . . . not actually, she admitted, inside my head, as if embarrassed.

"So where's Sister Marguerite, then?" I wondered.

The old woman frowned. "Unfortunately, she's been in a coma since the locust episode last year."

"The locust episode?"

"You don't want to know." She held up the flat of her hand. "Just trust me."

"And no one else in the Circle does vampires?"

The Bone Lady mustered a defiant look that did little to reassure me. "There aren't that many vampires," she said. "And besides, there is no one else."

"Well, how were you planning to do this on your own?"

"I'd planned on utilizing dynamite, but," she wrung her hands, "I just feel so . . . exhausted lately. I can't tell you how excited I was to stumble upon you, Svetlana. It's as if—"

"Dynamite?" *Whoa, whoa, whoa! What? What in the world are you talking about?*

"I realize dynamite would be an unorthodox app—"

"But where would you get it? Where would you find dynamite?"

"Oh, I have it," she said, nodding. "Quite a bit, actually—from an old contact in Nevada. Sister Marguerite and I closed the Portal to Hell several years ago and—"

"You have dynamite?" *Unbelievable,* I thought. But why would I think that? Here we were discussing vampires and ghouls and demonic portals—why should an old lady's secret stash of high explosives surprise me?

"I made contact with Mr. McAvoy prior to my arrival in Sunny Hill. He assured me the dynamite is completely viable, although somewhat unstable. He stressed the importance of using extreme caution. He retired from mining almost two decades ago, you see, so the material is quite old."

Unstable dynamite, I thought.

"It's just an option."

"And there's absolutely no one else to help us?"

Lenora Bones scratched through her gray curls with spidery fingers, biting down on her bottom lip in deep thought. "Marguerite's in her blasted coma, and Mrs. Matheson recently underwent hip surgery." She looked to the ceiling. "There's Constance Angelica, but she hasn't been heard from since the Qwerril uprising—"

"Qwerril?"

"Very nasty. I don't hold out much hope for Constance."

"But what about Daphne St. Simone?"

"Dead ten years now," she said, pinching her lips around a sad memory.

"But how many are there in the Circle of Red?"

"Including you . . ." She rolled her eyes in her head, counting. "Five. Assuming that Constance is alive."

The Circle of Red: She and I, Sister Marguerite (in a coma), Mrs. Matheson (recuperating from hip surgery), and Constance Angelica—assuming she was still alive. I felt my own shoulders slumping. I was suddenly tired to the bone. I had an urge to curl up on the floor and go to sleep. Instead, I reached into my trunk and pulled out two whips of red licorice, handing one over to Ms. Bones.

"I know it's daunting, dear," she said, a genuine smile finding its way to her face. She tugged at the licorice and chewed. *But it is our privilege to protect the weak. It doesn't seem it, I know, but even as old as I am and as young as you are, we are very powerful, Svetlana. Together we can do this.* Her gray eyes had softened and the cookie smell had strengthened around her. I breathed it in, the richness, of it and felt somewhat better. She stood from the chair, wincing against the popping stiffness of her joints. I reached my arms about her and gave a gentle hug, receiving one from her in return.

What are we going to do? I thought.

Lovely girl, she sent to me.

I kissed the tiny lady's wrinkled brow. *I don't want you sneaking up into this tree house anymore,* I insisted. *That's twice now.*

Twice that you know of, dear. She smirked, pulling off another bite of licorice. *And I'm not so frail as you might think.*

"I have no doubt," I said, pulling the top of her housecoat closed against the night air, covering the red stone at her throat.

But we must plan our attack, she whispered inside my mind, stooping to look through a window into the night. *We must confront the vampire and free the children before it's too late.*

Could she actually mean this moment? *Now?*

Certainly now—we have not a moment to waste. She turned from the window, her eyes leaping to life with a glowing resolve.

But I couldn't do this now. *If my parents wake up and I'm—*

We must act, Svetlana! She rapped the table with her closed fist, coming around, reaching and gripping my shoulders. *There is nothing else to consider, we must—*

But with the last word, she placed a careless footstep backward and dropped through the opening in the floor. She loosed a surprised cry and disappeared in a blink. I felt her panic inside my mind as she plummeted. Almost immediately, I heard the impact as she hit the ground below. Downstairs, inside the house, Razor erupted into furious barking. I scuttled down the wooden slats to the bottom of the tree and knelt next to the tiny woman. She was crying. I didn't know how I knew that her leg was broken, but I did.

Well, this is terribly embarrassing, she thought, great goose egg tears coming down her face.

Are you okay, Ms. Bones?

She shook her head, eyes squeezed tight. *I have bungled this to no end! I'm so sorry, dear girl! Dreadfully sorry!* She turned slightly, wincing in my arms. I felt the gasp inside my mind as a sharp pain shot up through her cracked leg.

I cradled her head in my lap, pushing gray curls from her face. I leaned over and kissed her papery cheeks and breathed in the rich aroma of cookies. Upstairs, my parent's bedroom light snapped on, and the dark silhouette of my father's head appeared in the window and then just as quickly disappeared. Razor barked and barked and a moment later the front porch light blinked into life.

This is so terrible, Ms. Bones thought. *I have made such a mess of this.* She rubbed her bony fingers up and down my arm, her wet eyes glistening in the fading moonlight. *I am so sorry, dear.*

"Shh," I whispered. "You're going to be fine."

I heard my father running up behind us.

Of course I'll be fine, sweet girl. But what about you?

Sixteen

After the paramedics arrived and loaded Ms. Bones into the ambulance, Mom guided me back into the house. I wanted to go with Dad to the hospital, but he wouldn't allow it. He left in his car, following the ambulance, which drove without its siren, blue and red lights strobing through the fading darkness along Cherry Street. Several neighbors stood watching from their front porches, huddled in housecoats and pajamas.

"I just want to go and make sure she's all right," I told Mom.

"I know, but your father will take care of everything." Mom gave me a hug and ruffled my hair. The lotion she wore tickled my nose, something cinnamony. She said, "I don't understand why Ms. Bones had to have her journal in the middle of the night." She shook her head and kissed my brow. "I'm sure she'll be fine."

After Dad had rushed outside and discovered us below the tree house, Ms. Bones stayed mostly silent except to tell him she was okay. She told him she might have injured her leg, wincing in discomfort more than a few times, half of it an act so she wouldn't have to say too much. She suggested a story in my thoughts, and I repeated it. I explained to Dad that Ms. Bones had lent me her travel journal that afternoon. But then she had been unable to sleep and had come for the book during the night, hoping to find it in the tree house, where I had told her I'd keep it.

"You must think it terribly strange," Ms. Bones said, coughing and wincing, staring with sincere embarrassment into my father's face. "It's just that I recalled an important detail I wished to record in its pages. I was afraid I might forget. I have a terrible memory, you know. I hate that I sleep so little at night. I hate all this trouble I've put you through."

"No, no," Dad had assured her, although he was obviously confused. "Just—please be still. An ambulance is on its way."

The old woman and I shared a secret glance.

Mom had come outside a few moments after that. Neither she nor Dad realized I'd been inside the tree house when Ms. Bones had fallen. They both assumed I'd gone outside once Razor began barking, just ahead of Dad.

Now, as I went back upstairs to my room, Mom asked, "Did you and Ms. Bones have a good visit yesterday?"

"Yeah, she was cool."

"And she didn't seem . . ." Mom tilted her head slightly, winking an eye, which was her way of saying "nut job."

"You mean like Grandma Grimm?" Who was my dad's mom, the one I was named after. The one I thought was a little loopy.

Mom frowned, but I could see in her eyes that she didn't mean it. "Don't be mean," she half-warned.

"I'm not! Ms. Bones isn't like Grandma Grimm at all—she's okay."

Mom made a shooing motion, encouraging me up the stairs and back to sleep. "Your father will fill us both in later."

And, surprisingly, I did return to sleep, but it was not restful sleep. I tossed and turned beneath the bed, chased by dark dreams. In my nightmares, Ms. Larch clutched after me with red-nailed talons. She laughed and cackled. Her teeth were transformed, becoming pointed and razor-sharp, like those of a shark. I stumbled through the blackness of sleep, falling again and again, finally tumbling out of the tree house and crashing, not onto the ground but onto a carpet of dead cardinals and goldfish. A sea of lifeless eyes, black and filmy. . . .

The rooster clock showed nearly noon when I finally jerked awake, trembling, cotton-mouthed, and starving. The first thing that popped into my head was Ms. Bones—how was she doing? Then the missing girls. Then fettuccine with red clam sauce, leftovers from last night's dinner.

My stomach growled.

"Your dad said Ms. Bones might have to stay in the hospital for a day or two," Mom said, pushing a warmed plate of red pasta across the table to me. I could hear Dad outside in the tree house banging with a hammer, fixing the trapdoor so that it shut automatically whenever anyone went in or out of the hideout.

"He should have done that before," Mom scolded, staring out the window.

But it was my fault, really, for never taking the time to shut the door behind me.

"What if Ms. Bones had broken her neck? Or, God forbid, it was you in the hospital with something broken."

"I'm careful," I said.

After I'd finished eating, I went outside. Dad was climbing down the wooden slats. He told me Ms. Bones had suffered a simple fracture of the fibula, which meant she'd cracked the bone in her lower leg above her foot. *Crack!* I hated the way that sounded. I winced, imagining my own leg bone cracking.

"The doctor said she might be able to come home tomorrow if there are no complications," Dad added. "I told her to telephone and I'd be happy to drive her home from the hospital when she's ready." He was arranging his tools inside the toolbox. He ran the sleeve of his sweaty shirt across his sweaty brow (Dad has glandular issues). "Geez," he sighed. "Imagine if that poor lady had fallen and broken her neck."

"She's not going to sue us, Dad," I said, trying to be funny, although the look on his face told me he didn't appreciate the joke.

He glanced up at the tree house. "You might be a bit too old for this thing anyway, Stephanie."

I let the name slide. "Too old to have my own space?"

"Oh, I don't mind that," he said. "I just don't think we can afford to have our neighbors falling out of trees like acorns." He lifted his toolbox and headed for the garage. "You might have to run some meals over to Ms. Bones over the next few weeks."

Which I'd be happy to do, I said, following after him.

"Poor old lady's got no family around here."

"I can do it."

He gave me a bright-eyed smile and said I was a good girl, which made me feel kind of like a jerk. What would Dad think if he knew I wasn't being completely honest about everything? I felt awful lying to him—and Mom, too—which was really what I was doing. Even if it wasn't lying exactly, just not telling them the entire truth.

I asked if it'd be all right if I went for a ride, and he said sure. I took off, pedaling up tree-lined Cherry Street. It was another nice day. There was a light breeze blowing, sunny skies above, happy people strolling up and down, beautiful birds whistling, butterflies floating from flower to flower. Picture-perfect: not the kind of world where monsters roamed, where sixth-grade science teachers snatched students and drained them of their blood.

Could Sandy Cross and her friends *really* still be alive? They'd been missing for three days now. The authorities continued to search the woods. "Missing" posters still fluttered on telephone poles—all to no effect. I tried to picture the three girls but couldn't. Where could they be hidden? Within Larch's lair? Wherever she lived had to be a lair! That seemed the likeliest place to start, although I had no idea where that was.

But I knew how I might find out.

One thing was for sure: I had to come up with a plan. Everything was up to me now, wasn't it? Ms. Bones had broken her leg and wouldn't be any immediate help— even after she returned home from the hospital. Tomorrow or the next day, it didn't matter. Besides being a million years old, she was incapacitated. And she'd said so herself: the Kensington Vampire had to be stopped now, before anyone else fell into her clutches.

I pedaled back up Cherry Street, slowing before I reached my house. I ducked into the Bone Lady's driveway, pushing my bike to the rear of the brick house. My eyes darted to the spot where the cardinal had died, but the poor bird was gone. I imagined that Ms. Bones had buried the tiny thing. Poisoned! When all along I had been the intended victim!

The back door to the house was unlocked, and I slipped inside. The place was silent, filled with the lingering pleasantness of the old woman's warm-cookie smell. I made my way through the near-empty rooms, tiptoeing, lifting an ear to listen. The den was filled with mostly unopened boxes. The upstairs bedroom was nearly bare, with only a narrow bed pushed against the wall and a pair of black shoes in the corner. Black binoculars rested on the windowsill. The view was over the fence into my own front yard. I saw the tree house and Dad washing our car in the driveway. Razor sat in the middle of the yard, looking up at me in the window. He cocked his head curiously, but didn't bark. *Good boy,* I thought, and waved.

Back downstairs, in the garage, a compact car sat in

dusty silence. A pair of fuzzy dice hung from the rearview mirror. A bumper sticker read: HONK IF YOU LOVE GARLIC. Against the garage wall, a rake, a shovel, and a broom hung from brackets beside a door that opened onto a basement staircase.

A switch at the top of the steps brought a light bulb into dull life below. The wooden stairway creaked beneath my black sneakers. I stepped down into the cold. It was like entering a refrigerator. The walls of the basement faded into shadow beyond the reach of the dangling bulb. A Styrofoam ice chest rested on the concrete floor.

I waited in the half-light at the bottom of the steps and listened; there was no sound from anywhere. I knelt next to the cooler and removed the lid. The sudden squeak of Styrofoam was unbearably loud, and I winced. I moved my head aside to allow the slight light to fall into the container. Inside, there was a wooden mallet and two wooden stakes laid across a square of sackcloth. The stakes were each a foot in length, sawed-off sections of oak, as thick as a broom handle. They were sharpened to a clean point at one end and sawed flat at the other, to take the strike of the mallet. I shivered with ... what? Dread? Fear? Excitement? Or was it anticipation? My hands trembled as I reached and rolled up the mallet and stakes into the sackcloth and lifted them from the cooler. The remainder of the cooler was stacked full with clay-colored rods.

When everything was laid out, I counted twenty-two sticks of dynamite.

Seventeen

With my backpack filled and hanging heavily off my shoulders, I rode down Stallings Street looking for Fumio Chen's house, the one with the tacky silver gazing ball balanced in the front yard. I found it and leaned my bike against the porch railing. I pushed the doorbell, and a faint *Bong-bong-bong* sounded within.

The girl who answered must have been his older sister. She hardly gave me a glance, turning and yelling "Fumio!" before disappearing back inside. He arrived a moment later, still dressed in what must have been his church clothes. Amazingly, he looked even less cool than usual. I frowned at his black pants and brown shoes and almost said something but managed to hold my tongue.

"Hey, Svet."

"You're not supposed to wear brown shoes with black pants," I blurted, unable to help myself.

"Why not?" Fumio looked blankly down at his shoes.

If a tree falls in the forest, does anybody hear it? I mean, if no one's there? To hear it, I mean? Whatever. "Listen, I'm sorry." And I was. I wasn't interested in butting heads with Fumio or getting into a verbal tussle—I needed his help, and that's exactly what I told him.

"Now, you know I'm not a licensed mental-health professional, right?" He showed me a mouthful of braces and rubber bands.

He was so clever. Ha-ha. "Listen," I said. "This is for your benefit, too. You want to be a reporter, right?"

"I am a reporter."

"That's what I mean—you *are* a reporter. So we can help each other out, see?"

"Is this about Ms. Larch trying to kill you?"

"Just holster the questions for now, Lois Lane. We'll round up your friend Jimmy Olsen, and I'll fill you both in then. But first, you better change out of those sharp threads—and I suggest a pair of running shoes."

Fumio rolled his eyes but came outside a few minutes later changed from his church clothes into shorts and a T-shirt. We pedaled over to Dwight Foote's place on Mango Court. The house looked like some kind of mansion. There was a spouting fountain in the front yard like the kind at the mall that dingbat people throw coins into. The famous Foote Family bird feeders were in the front yard, too, along with bushes sculpted into animal shapes and three—count 'em, three!—ultra-tacky gazing balls. Two stone lions with attitude crouched on pedestals at the end of the driveway, one on either side of the opened gate. Pretty ritzy.

We followed the winding drive up to the open garage doors, where Foote was patching the front tire on his bike. "Had a nail in it," he said, lifting his big head and grinning.

I whistled at the three fancy-pants luxury cars lined up inside the enormous garage. "Didn't know you were rich, Foote."

"My dad's a cardiologist," he explained, tightening the bolts on the wheel.

"That's a heart doctor," Fumio offered.

"Duh," I said.

Foote clamped on an air hose and began pumping up the tire. He asked what we were up to.

"Svetlana wants to stalk Ms. Larch," Fumio said.

I balled up my fist, and Fumio stepped away. "I just want you guys to show me where she lives."

"What for?" Foote asked.

"You'll see. And you don't have to do anything but show me." I slid my thumbs under my backpack straps, easing the pressure off my shoulders. The bag seemed to be getting heavier. "You think I'm crazy, so what's the big deal?"

Foote said, "We'd be accessories to your insanity."

"Yeah," Fumio added. "We'll be enabling you."

Oh, brother. "You need to lay off the Oprah, brace-face."

"Ms. Larch wasn't driving that van yesterday," Foote said. "You saw that. Nobody's trying to kill you."

"All you've got to do is show me where her house is."

"And then what are you going to do?" Foote wondered.

"Then I'll see," I said. "I'll look around. Even if she wasn't in the van yesterday, don't you think it's worth a look? What about the missing girls? I'm telling you, there's more to Ms. Larch than meets the eye."

Fumio said, "You're a riot, you know that?"

"If you're a reporter, then you need to learn to follow your nose," I told him. "My nose can run circles around yours, easy. But I'll give you a snoop lesson—free of charge. Worst-case scenario, you've still got a great story. I'll even give you the headline: 'New Girl Goes Off Deep End.'"

Fumio shook his head, but he was smiling. "Dwight," he said. "Go get your camera."

Eighteen

Fumio Chen had an idea of where Larch lived because of the story he'd written about her for the *Sunny Hill Bee*. Or at least he thought he did. Somewhere along Culver Point Road, a dirt track that dead-ended at the Flint River.

"There aren't many houses out there," he said.

"Just get me close." I had a pretty good idea I'd figure out which was hers. I was counting on my nose and the foul stench of the Kensington Vampire.

Culver Point Road was on the far side of City Park, where I'd never been before. The sun was still hanging in the sky, but already it was creeping up on six o'clock. Foote and Fumio didn't seem concerned by the hour. I knew I wouldn't be making it home in time for Sunday dinner, but I couldn't worry about that. Maybe I'd already eaten my last meal and didn't even know it. But that wasn't being very positive.

My parents were going to kill me, anyway.

Culver Point Road started off paved, but soon turned into gravel, then sand. There weren't many houses along the road, just as Fumio had said. And after a while, there were none. The thin tires on my bicycle didn't do well in the sand. The heavy backpack dug into my shoulders. Foote offered to tote it for a while, but if he and Fumio found out what I was hauling, they'd bug out in a panic.

More than a small part of me thought turning tail wasn't such a bad idea. Instead, I said, "Are you sure Larch lives out here?" I was beginning to think that maybe Fumio didn't know where he was going. I hadn't picked up a whiff of anything remotely evil.

"When I interviewed her, she said she liked living near the river. That's got to be the Flint River, so that's got to be this road. There aren't any houses along the river, except out here. At least not in town."

"Maybe it's one of the houses we already passed," Foote said, ready to turn back.

"But the river's up ahead," Fumio noted.

I said, "I'll know her place if it's out here." I had no doubt of that.

Fumio was watching me. "What do you think you've got? Some kind of psychic power?"

"No," I fibbed, "just a bad feeling." To the bone.

Through the woods, the river was beginning to appear and disappear, winding closer to the dirt road. Birds tittered and flitted in the branches crisscrossing the tract of sky overhead. All around, everything was being swallowed in shadows. Sunlight was dwindling as the road narrowed and the woods closed in.

"Let's come back and do this tomorrow after school," Foote suggested, looking nervously at the fading light.

The day suddenly seemed to be draining away, almost sucked away. Sweat soaked through my shirt where the backpack pressed between my shoulder blades. The chain on Fumio's bike squeaked. Spokes creaked. Wheels crunched and shushed over gravel and sand. Up ahead, the road curved around a bend and out of sight. Through the trees, I made out the shape of a lone house.

All three of us swung off our bikes and stood at the side of the road, silently peering through the woods. I became aware of the murmuring of the river moving unseen beyond the bend. There was only that and the sound of our breathing. The birdsong had ceased. Leaves hung motionless in the still air. I pushed my bike forward.

"Hey, this is the end of the road," Foote whispered.

I looked over my shoulder, and he was waving at me to come back. He blinked, but his eyes didn't look blue now, they looked gray in the dying light. The shoulder sling was gone from his arm today, but the plaster cast ran from elbow to fingers. I could make out scribbles of black marker where friends had written on his cast. He'd asked me to sign it, but I was too cool for that. Now it didn't seem like such a big deal. I should have signed it. "You two wait here," I whispered back.

Fumio hissed, "Don't go!"

I pushed my bike into the bushes and laid it down. I didn't stop to think. I knew if I did, I'd chicken out. I crunched ahead over dead leaves and branches, stooped, watching the house grow bigger as I edged my way through the underbrush. I could see where the dirt road wound around and ended at the front of the two-story structure. The last house on a dead-end street. It seemed to fit the bill—the kind of place where something bad could happen.

The house was weathered, built of worn wood. Despite its size, it seemed almost to lean backward, as if it might slide down through the trees and into the river behind it. A two-car garage was attached at the side. I made out the corner of a wide deck on the back of the house. The land sloped away from the porch, leading to the shadowed river beyond the trees and a rickety dock leaning on stilts in the water. I crept forward and halted at the edge of the neglected yard, flinching as a thorny bramble scratched my cheek. I knelt in the bushes, resting my knuckles in the dirt, watching.

I smelled the rot. It could have been some poor possum or lonely raccoon, some tired animal that had curled up and died, but it wasn't. This was her place—the Lair of the Kensington Vampire. Ms. Larch's Dark Abode. Diana Frost's Fortress of Despair. You get the idea. There was no doubt in my mind. A round knocker in the center of the front door spied like a watchful eye. The windows were shuttered with dark curtains. A mildewed tarp covered an abandoned vehicle parked alongside the house. Thirsty plants wilted half-dead in pots lining the front stoop and walkway.

So now what? I shrugged off my backpack. Could the front door be unlocked? Not likely, but I wouldn't know unless I tried. Maybe I should try a window first? That would be best—sneak around and see if I could peek through a window. Maybe find one I could push open and slip through. The house seemed empty, felt empty. Only the rotted smell told me that Sylvia Larch lived there.

Could the missing girls be inside? Just within those walls, only feet from where I stood? And what would I do if Ms. Larch were indeed inside right now? I looked to the row of dusty windows along the top of the garage door. The windows were too high to peek through. But if I stood on something, I could peer inside; I could turn over one of the potted plants and stand on that. If her car was in the garage, then I'd know she was home. The car beneath the tarp clearly wasn't hers. The mildewed plastic was heaped with dead leaves, and the vehicle had obviously not been used for some time.

I ran across the shadowed yard in a crouch, holding my pack in my arms. I stood with my back pressed against the garage door, as if balancing along a narrow ledge. I stared back through the woods but couldn't make out Foote and Fumio. They'd probably run off—cowards! I didn't need them anyway. But wait, there they were. I saw them now. They were looking down the road, as if distracted.

I bit back a shriek as the garage door suddenly jerked into life behind me. The paneled door started to rise, squealing and clunking as it cranked up from the concrete drive. I dashed away from the opening door, snatching up my bag, twenty-two sticks of dynamite swinging wildly in my grasp. I saw Fumio and Foote bolt into the woods, scrambling away from the dirt road as a white van barreled into sight, trailing a thick cloud of dust. I plunged into the bushes as the van wheeled around the bend and slowed, then pulled into the darkened garage. Doors opened and closed inside the garage, and then there was nothing. The garage door remained open. I made out the back of the parked van, and beside it, the back of a dark sports car— Larch's car.

"Psst!" Fumio spit, crawling up behind me. "Let's get out of here!" He tugged at my shoulder.

I swatted his hand away and told him to be quiet.

Foote crunched up through the bushes and said enough was enough. "Let's go, guys," he insisted, obviously rattled.

"That's the white van from yesterday," I said.

"You don't know that!" Fumio snapped.

"The other car in the garage is the one Ms. Larch was driving."

"Fine," Foote said. "You can call the cops when we get home." He had his big head near mine in the bushes. He looked awfully nervous, but at least he didn't seem to be thinking about kissing me today. And nervous was definitely an understatement—he looked scared witless.

The same as Fumio.

The same as me, I had no doubt.

"C'mon, guys, it's gonna be dark soon," Fumio said, his voice cracking.

He was right, but that just meant we needed to hurry. I hitched my pack onto my shoulders and rushed across the yard toward the house. I heard the sharp intake of breath behind me as I left.

"Don't!" Fumio groaned after me.

I raced, bent over, and crouched down next to the tarp-covered car. My heart thudded behind my chestbone, the wild beat pounding in my neck and ears. I slunk around to the end of the tarp as Foote and Fumio rushed up.

Foote begged in a whisper, "Please, Svet, let's call this off."

Fumio lifted up the edge of the tarp and let out a low whistle. "Check it out," he breathed, raising the tarp even higher. It was the front end of a canary-yellow Corvette. The exposed vanity plate read: SCI-GUY. "This is Mr. Boyd's car!"

The missing science teacher! The one who had "skipped town"! The one Ms. Larch had replaced! But I didn't understand . . .

"He must be who's driving the van!" Foote declared, too loudly.

I frowned, squeezing his arm and shushing him. I leaned forward and spied around the corner to the front of the house. No lights had come on in any of the windows. No sound came from inside. It looked as if the garage door was still open. This close to the house, the smell of rot was stifling. My skin tingled all over; warning bells screamed inside my head like a fire alarm.

"Hey, guys—" Fumio started.

"Maybe you're right, Svet," Foote said.

"Guys—"

"Maybe Larch *is* mixed up in something."

"Guys, look—"

"Maybe she and Mr. Boyd are up to no good."

"Guys—I don't think Mr. Boyd's been up to anything lately." Fumio finally got his words out.

He'd dragged the tarp completely off the hood of the Corvette and was staring through the windshield at a dead guy propped up in the driver's seat.

It was definitely a dead guy.

I was looking at a dead guy.

I really needed to swallow, but my throat had turned to sandpaper, dry as a bone.

Thunk Thunk Thunk Thunk Thunk.

My heart galloped like a champion racehorse. It beat so hard it hurt.

The body behind the steering wheel hardly seemed real. It looked like a skeleton—or a mummy—wrinkled like a prune, and leathery. It was just bones and skin, deflated, the life leaked out of it—or sucked out of it.

"Mr. Boyd . . ." Foote whispered. He walked up to the car window like a zombie and peered inside. The sunken face had a weird leer frozen on it. Its eyes were invisible behind mirrored sunglasses. The brown mop of hair looked like a wig. "It's him." Foote slowly lifted a finger and tapped the glass.

Fumio said, "Trust me, he's not gonna hear you."

A sharp banging sound came from somewhere inside the house, and we ducked back down, huddled like puppies inside a cardboard box, shivering. I peered around the corner, but there was still no movement.

"I'm out of here," Fumio said.

"No," I said. "We've got to go inside."

Foote didn't say anything. He just reached back with his good arm and punched me hard on the shoulder.

"Jerk!" I said.

"You're the jerk!"

Fumio said, "You *are* a jerk, Svetlana. There's no freaking way we're going in there."

I threw my thumb at the Corvette. "*That* proves I'm right."

"That proves this is a job for the cops," he said.

"You boneheads don't get it. Larch is a monster!" I nodded at the body behind the wheel. "That guy was bled dry. Vampire food. Larch drained your old science teacher and took his job. She wants to turn Sunny Hill Middle School into a giant kid buffet." I looked from one frightened face to the other. "She can't be arrested—she's not even human."

"There's nothing we can do about it!" Fumio insisted.

"We're the only ones that can do anything," I said. "If the cops come swarming up here, she's just going to escape—even if they catch her, she'll get away. She could turn into a bat for all we know. And if she gets away, there'll be no stopping her." I sounded like Lenora Bones now, and I knew everything I said was true. I breathed in deep, the sickening rot spoiling the air. I sucked in the evil—and hated it.

I grabbed Foote and Fumio by their wrists and squeezed. *You've got to help me,* I thought, directing the command into their stunted, masculine brains. *We must destroy Sylvia Larch.* I bored my psychic command into their thick skulls, willing them to obey. "We must destroy the Kensington Vampire."

"You want us to . . . kill our science teacher?"

"She's already dead—we just need to stop her."

"But what can we do?"

I shrugged off my backpack and unzipped it. I pulled out the bundled sackcloth and unrolled it, displaying the pointed stakes and mallet.

"No way," Foote groaned.

I opened the bag wider, revealing the dynamite that filled the rest of the pack.

"You're a psycho," Fumio breathed.

Foote said, "I don't want you to be my girlfriend anymore."

Nineteen

I crawled on my hands and knees along the ground in front of the house. The daylight had turned to dusk. It was still light in the orange-streaked sky, but it was dark in the surrounding woods, and getting darker by the moment. Dad would certainly be angry by now wondering where I was. Mom would be worried. I looked over my shoulder at Foote and Fumio crawling behind me. Fumio carried a stake and mallet. Foote gripped the other stake in his good fist.

I peeked into the opened garage. The space was dark, crowded with the van and the sports car. It stank of oil and dust and underlying rot. I duck-walked between the vehicles. The door leading into the house was closed. At the rear of the garage, stacked against a freezer, three bikes leaned in the shadows—girls' bikes. I stood quietly and pointed out the bicycles as the two boys tiptoed inside behind me. Their eyes grew wide in the half-light.

"Holy—" Fumio began and didn't finish.

Foote said, "The two red ones are Marsha's and Madison's—the same bikes, the same baskets, everything."

"What if they're like . . . Mr. Boyd?" Fumio whispered. He held the mallet raised, ready to swing in an instant.

I couldn't think about the girls being like Mr. Boyd. The Bone Lady had said that a vampire might take weeks to drain a victim. I dropped to my knees and unzipped my backpack. The dynamite smelled like wet cardboard. I reached inside. The sticks were damp, sweating. They were hot from being inside the bag strapped across my back. Ms. Bones had kept the dynamite in the basement of her house inside an ice chest to keep it cool. It was a bad thing when old dynamite began to overheat. It became unstable. It began to sweat nitroglycerin.

I was sweating, too.

What if this bag of explosives blew up right in my face? That would be a fine plan. The blast might still destroy Sylvia Larch, but it wouldn't save the girls—if they could be saved—and it certainly wouldn't be pleasant for the boys. Or me.

"What?" Foote whispered, wondering what I was doing.

"I'm going to leave this dynamite out here," I said softly, indicating the bag.

"What if we need it," Fumio asked.

"Can't use it in the house anyway—not while we're inside. Plus it's unstable."

"Great, you're a perfect match, then," Fumio said.

"Put it inside the freezer," Foote suggested.

I looked at the freezer behind the bikes. That wasn't a bad idea. It was about the size of a refrigerator knocked over on its side. It was old, off-white, with a thick door over it like a giant lid. My grandma had one just like it in her basement in Texas. She kept it filled with hamburger meat and ribs. I reached for the silver handle and hesitated. What was this freezer filled with? I glanced at the bikes leaning against it. They were already gathering dust. What if the girls were . . .?

I opened the freezer lid. A burp of foul air wafted out, warm and musty. I wrinkled my nose at the rank smell. The freezer was empty, not even working. It was warmer inside the old box than it was inside the garage. I couldn't leave the dynamite in there.

"Gross," Fumio said. "Shut that stinking thing."

I quietly closed the lid. I set the backpack of dynamite on the garage floor and pushed it beneath the van, where it would be hidden and out of the way. Foote had moved over to the closed door leading into the house. He had his ear pressed against it, listening. No light shone from under it. He shook his head to show he didn't hear anything. I made a "gimme" gesture to Fumio and took the stake and mallet from him. He gave them up easily.

I motioned to Foote, and he turned the doorknob slowly. The door clicked open. As it swung inward, a terrified look fell over his face. I gritted my teeth, imagining the door creaking wildly, screeching open on rusted hinges, but it eased open in a yawning silence. Cold air washed into the garage.

I stepped through the doorway into a shadow-filled laundry room. A washing machine and dryer were pushed against the wall. Shelves were stacked with bleach bottles and detergent boxes. An open doorway led into the kitchen. Another door was closed. Light came from under it—and so did the sugary scent of bubblegum.

I pointed. "There."

Foote pulled the door open. I pushed him and his big head out of the way. A dozen concrete steps led down into a lighted basement. The bubblegum smell was strong: Not as strong as the rotting smell—but definitely there. I eased down the steps. My scalp tingled as I descended. The edge of a table came into sight. Then two shoes, two legs, two hands, and finally the whole of Sandy Cross and her mass of blond hair. Beyond her were two more tables—Madison laid out on one and Marsha on the other. Or maybe it was the other way around. I couldn't tell which was which. They were flat on their backs.

"Are they . . . ?"

"No," I said to Foote, who'd crept halfway down the steps after me. I saw that the girls were still breathing, although they made no other movement. Each was laid out on a metal table, looking asleep, although they weren't sleeping—they'd have woken up by now if they were.

"I can't believe it," Foote said.

"What?" Fumio's urgent whisper came from the top of the stairs.

The girls were all slack-faced, their breathing shallow,

their eyes closed. They had on the same clothes they'd been wearing when I'd last seen them, Thursday after school. Ladybug earrings dangled from each earlobe.

"Are they drugged?" Foote wondered.

"What is it?" Fumio asked from above.

"Tell him to bring down some bleach," I told Foote. I slid the wooden stake into my belt, setting the mallet aside. I shook Sandy's shoulders, and she grumbled. "Wake up," I said. Her face wrinkled into a frown and then went slack again. "Wake up." I shook harder. She moaned and I patted her on the cheek. "Wake up, loser."

Just the sight of her put me in a bad mood.

Each of the girls had a gauze bandage taped inside the crook of her arm—just like a person who had donated blood. Only nobody around here was donating. I slapped Sandy's face harder. "Snap out of it, Sleeping Beauty."

"Take it easy," Foote said, coming back down the steps with wide-eyed Fumio in tow. Fumio at least had a jug of bleach with him.

"You take it easy," I said. "We need to get out of here, or we're all going to end up on these tables."

"Holy smokes," Fumio marveled, staring at the girls. "You were freaking right."

I grabbed the bleach and tilted a chin toward Marsha and Madison. "Start waking up those two." Sandy's eyelids fluttered as I unscrewed the bleach cap. "C'mon, you," I said. I poured a few drops of bleach into the cap and held it under her nose. She sputtered and turned her head. I followed with the cap, and she coughed and swatted at my hand. Her eyes winced against the light. "Get up, bonehead."

She gagged, pushing my hand away, then sat up coughing. "Ugh," she moaned. She shook her bob of nightmarish blond hair and balled fists into her eyes, rubbing. "Aaaghth," she slobbered. She wiped drool from the corner of her mouth.

Nice.

Fumio and Foote were bringing the other two around. "Give me some of that bleach," Foote said.

Sandy Cross yawned and then hacked. She looked about the room, her pale face twisted into an ugly mask. Her hair was a blond wreck. She had lumps of dried sleep in the corners of her eyes. She made that awful "aaaghth" sound again. She glared around the room, taking it in, taking us in.

"This isn't the Food Court," she croaked.

Twenty

It was cruel fate having to save these bimbos. What a bunch of complainers! Geez, with the questions—*blah, blah, blah!* And Fumio couldn't keep that blasted mouth of his shut! Going on about shriveled-up Mr. Boyd outside in his Corvette. Could the load of them possibly make a louder racket? What was this, group amnesia? Did everyone just forget that there was a bloodthirsty vampire in the house?

"Shut up!" I hissed.

The girls climbed off their tables, looking as confused and mean as wet cats. And looking at us as if the whole thing was our fault.

They didn't have a clue.

"What's going on?" Sandy practically shouted.

I grabbed her by the shoulders. "Shh!"

She pushed me away and stumbled backward, glancing at the bandage across her arm. She poked the red-stained gauze with a finger. Her angry expression melted into concern. "Where are we?" she asked, looking up.

"Oh, man," Fumio said, rolling his eyes. "You don't want to know."

"I'm starving," Marsha said.

"Yeah," Madison chimed in.

This from two girls who could have easily passed for a pair of chopsticks, for two talking soda straws. Of course they were starving! They'd been starving since birth!

Sandy Cross was taking notice of the metal tables now. "What is this place?"

"You're in Larch's basement," Foote told her.

Sandy frowned. "Ms. Larch—our teacher?"

"We just saw Ms. Larch—" Marsha began.

"At the mall," Madison finished.

"Well, you ain't in the mall no more," Fumio said. "Larch put the mojo on you."

I snapped my fingers and told him to get the girls out of here. "C'mon, let's get moving." Marsha and Madison opened their beaks to squawk, but I froze them with a stare. "There's no time for catch up now—just get up the stairs."

"Ketchup?" Madison said.

Oh, boy.

I told Fumio to get the girls on their bikes and get them down the road ASAP. "Just get everyone out of here. Call the cops when you reach somebody's house."

Foote sighed. "*Now* she wants to call the cops."

Fumio said, "What are you two going to do?"

I lifted the mallet from the table. "We're gonna look around."

Twenty-one

I pulled aside a heavy curtain in the living room and peeked out the window. Beyond the smudged glass, the girls pushed their bikes away from the house and followed Fumio around the bend in the road. They were each staring back over their shoulders, their pale faces indistinct in the gathering gloom. Then they were gone, swallowed in the trees. It was too dark to see through the woods now, the sun had fled.

Foote crouched wearily in the center of the room, looking toward the worn steps and banister leading upstairs. The living room was drenched in murky shadow, spotted with the dark shapes of furniture. End tables bracketed a couch. There was a low coffee table. A desk butted up against a wall. A grandfather clock loomed silently, its pendulum hanging dead. Dusty lamps hunched, unlit. Enormous paintings tilted crooked on the walls.

I surveyed the silence and rot, my eyes finally following the banister up.

I pointed to the stairs, and Foote frowned, shaking his head.

I pointed.

He shook.

I pointed.

His face scrunched into a pained expression. "Let's go," he whispered. Meaning leave.

This was going to be like pulling teeth, but I needed his help. I slid the stake from my belt and tightened my grip on the mallet. The hammer was heavy. The stake was thick, like the fat end of a pool cue. The wood point had been shaven sharp. The weapons felt good in my hands. They filled me with a confidence that I didn't dare let waver. If for a moment I allowed fear to take hold, I would be strangled in its grip.

I nodded once more toward the stairway, and Foote once more stubbornly refused.

Useless.

I tiptoed softly across the carpet. Must, dust, and decay filled my nose. The rotting smell was strong at the bottom of the stairs. I eased my foot onto the first step; it creaked. I could *feel* Foote wince behind me. I ascended slowly, as if moving through molasses. The steps made little mouse noises beneath my feet. The stench of decay ripened as I climbed.

Thankfully, Foote started up after me. He was a jerk, but not entirely.

I paused on the top step. A darkened corridor ran the

length of the second floor. The window at the end of the hallway was curtained off. Two closed doors faced each other on either side of the hall. A dim light glowed beneath the door on the left. I crept forward and bent at the keyhole; there was only a flickering blackness inside. I rested my hand on the doorknob. Beside me, Foote shook his head furiously. He mouthed the word "No," but I turned the handle anyway. There was a slight metal click as the latch freed itself. The door swung inward.

A stifling stench roiled outward. I flinched against the foul wave of putrid air. On the far side of the dimly lit room, a four-poster bed was positioned against the wall. A billowing red canopy hung from the ceiling. Ms. Larch lay face-up on the covers, asleep. Candlelight flickered at a bedside table, the slender taper nearly finished, melted down to a waxy puddle. The dying light played across her alabaster skin. Shadows writhed in the room, uncoiling like snakes.

I shrugged off Foote's gripping fingers and eased through the doorway. Half of me wanted to flee, to drop the stake and mallet and run screaming. But that was only half. The rest of me wanted to destroy, to squash Larch like a bug, to crush her like a disgusting spider. That was the reason I was here. The very sight of her filled me with dread—with anger borne of self-preservation. I wanted to protect myself—to protect everyone. I wanted to lash out. I wanted to stop her. She was a monster. She was hideous and foul and . . . beautiful.

Her skin was unblemished, snowy white. Her raven hair spread like a glossy pillow around her perfectly sculpted face. Her long neck, her long fingers, and her long legs were the shapely design of a goddess. A sleek dress sheathed her supermodel body in silken black. Her lips were full, and red. A pulse jumped in her luminous throat, pumping stolen blood, corrupted blood. Her mouth was stained, like a Kool-Aid stain—but not with Kool-Aid. A drinking glass on the bedside table was black at the bottom. Black with dried blood.

I shivered.

Foote trembled beside me, gawking over Larch's blood-drunk body. I slid the wooden stake I was holding back into my belt and pointed at the stake in Foote's grasp.

The look on his face said: What?

I jabbed my finger at his stake and then tapped my chest.

Again: What?

OMG!

I tapped my chest and pointed to Larch's chest. I gripped the mallet handle with both hands and hefted it above my head. Foote stepped away. I flashed him a look of raw fury. I bared my teeth. *"Do it!"* I mouthed, silently, willing him to step forward. I was ready to whack *him* with the mallet if he didn't.

He held the stake out. The sharpened length wavered in his trembling hands. His shoulders trembled. His lips trembled. His knees trembled. His eyes, wide with fear, *blink-blink-blinked* behind heavy glasses. Reflected candle-light danced in the thick lenses. He lifted the stake over Larch, the deadly point quivering only inches above the left side of her chest.

Grr . . .

His dad was a freaking cardiologist! And Foote didn't even know where the heart was! I wanted to drop the mallet on his stupid head. "Over," I breathed.

Foote furrowed his brow, then realizing his error, moved the stake so it was centered over her chest.

Geez.

I swallowed. I'd have to pound with all my might to hammer the stake through bone. Could I even do it? And what if I missed? The mallet felt like stone in my hands, so heavy. My palms were slick with sweat. I focused on the quivering stake. It blurred. I squeezed my eyes shut and opened them. Larch's face floated below me like a white mask. The candle sputtered. The pulse in her neck throbbed with the beating of her heart.

Thump-thump.

Thump-thump.

Thump-thump.

"C'mon," Foote whimpered.

But I couldn't do it. My arms had turned to jelly. My willpower had dissolved. The mallet shook in my hands. I'd been rigid as steel, but now I was rubber. I wanted to melt away, the same as the sputtering candle.

Do it! I shouted inside my brain, commanding myself to act.

I raised the mallet higher

DO IT!

The door across the corridor clicked open, and suddenly Mr. Dumloch appeared, standing there in his pajamas. He filled the doorway, horrible and fat, yawning and scratching. I was frozen over Larch, poised to strike. Foote gulped guiltily and pulled the stake away, almost embarrassed. Dumloch looked up from his scratching, startled, then confused. Then he came roaring, bounding into the room, his fat rippling all around him as he rushed at us.

Foote screamed and backed away, waving the point of the stake in front of him.

On the bed, Larch's brilliant green eyes snapped opened. *Svetlana!* Her voice bloomed inside my head. *What a surprise!*

I jerked up the mallet, but it was too late. Her talon fingers locked on to my wrist and squeezed like steel tentacles. The mallet dropped, thudding to the floor. I was forced to my knees as she twisted my arm roughly. My cheek pressed into the rug. She twisted harder. I thought for a moment my shoulder would pop free of its socket. The pain was searing, an electric shock running the length of my arm.

Dumloch had snatched Foote into a powerful bear hug. The wooden stake dropped from Foote's hand. He hollered, writhing against Dumloch's grip. The history teacher lifted him off the floor like a sack of laundry.

"What in the world are you doing slinking around my bedroom, Mr. Foote?" Larch purred. She gave my wrist a vicious twist, and I yelped. Hot tears leapt to my eyes. "What terrible tales has Little Miss Grimm put into your giant, empty head?"

The smell of rot and dirty carpet filled my nose. Larch's red-painted toenails were in my face. Her grip tightened. I gritted my teeth against another painful twist.

Larch wagged a finger at Foote. "What were you going to do with that terrible toothpick, little man? You don't want a failing grade in my class, do you?" She giggled, a wet sound bubbling up from her dark heart. "You surely don't want an unsatisfactory mark on your permanent record." She jerked a thumb to the heavy drapes hanging against the wall, speaking to Dumloch. "I think Mr. Foote needs to be . . . expelled."

I squeezed my eyes shut. The stench of decay suffocated me. I cried out inside, the silent scream bursting from every cell, splitting me, half madness and half rage. The cry filled my head like a white light. I mustered my strength and jerked with all my might, snatching my hand free from the teacher's grip.

Foote was screaming, too, quite audibly, and flailing as Dumloch carried him across the room. At the window, Dumloch grunted, hurling Foote through the air into the closed curtains. Glass shattered behind the dark material, and both Foote and the drapes disappeared. Dumloch leaned out the broken window and peered at the ground below. "He's still moving," he said.

"Then go outside and *unmove* him," Larch commanded.

I jumped to my feet, sprinting for the doorway, but Larch snagged the collar of my shirt, pulling me backward, spinning me into Dumloch's waiting arms.

"Don't be in such a rush," she cooed. "Why invite yourself over if you're just going to run off?"

Dumloch lifted me from the floor. I was locked in his

beefy embrace. I was smothered against his chest. The stink of cheap cologne came off him in a wave and, beneath it, the underlying stench of spoiled meat. He was one of them, his blood turned, corrupted. A vampire.

I thrashed against his hold.

"*Tsk, tsk, tsk,*" Ms. Larch began. "You don't know whether to stay or go, do you?"

"Be still," Dumloch ordered, squeezing me tighter.

I punched against his wide chest. The foulness wafting off him sickened me. I kicked my legs. I thrashed. I was electrified with fear. If I could just break free of his grasp . . .

"What a nuisance you are," Larch said. She'd crossed her arms and was tapping her foot in mock impatience, frowning as I convulsed in Dumloch's idiot grip. "Is she more than you can handle, Cecil?"

Cecil?

"Fat lot of help you are," Dumloch complained.

I wrestled against his tarantula hold. I tugged a hand free and brought it hard across Dumloch's stubbled face, the force of it stinging my palm. His red jowls wobbled. He grinned, and I slapped again, harder. He laughed. I felt a jabbing in my side and remembered the stake I'd slipped into my belt earlier. I snatched it free and stabbed downward with all my strength. The wood point sank into his shoulder, and he roared in pain and surprise. His grip loosened, and I dropped to the floor.

Sylvia Larch laughed now.

I scrambled to my feet and bolted.

"Don't go," she called, her laughter chasing after me.

I heard her tell Dumloch not to just stand there bleeding.

I burst from the bedroom and lurched in a panic down the corridor toward the stairway. I slipped and stumbled down the steps, hugging the banister. Downstairs, I hit the floor running. I banged my shin, grimacing at the white-hot shock of pain, tumbled over the coffee table, and sprawled headlong across the living room floor. Somewhere a switch flipped and the dark house snapped into brilliance, every light in every room erupting into electric life. Footfalls landed heavily on the stairway behind me. I scampered on hands and knees into the kitchen.

Svetlana?

I tried to shut the invading voice from my mind.

Don't be shy.

A mechanical rumbling began. It was the automatic garage door closing. *No!* I jumped to my feet and ran. I slid across the laundry room floor and leapt through the doorway and over the stone steps into the garage. The steel door was rattling down. I crashed into the side of the white van and scuttled for the shrinking opening, diving and rolling. I slammed into the bottom of the garage door just as the metal met the floor.

Trapped!

Svetlana!

I fumbled to my feet, racing back toward the doorway, but Larch and Dumloch were already approaching. A shadow fell through the doorway into the garage from the laundry room. I cringed and bumped against the freezer. I opened the freezer door and let myself fall inside, dropping down into the suffocating funk. I pulled the door closed behind me. The trapped air was noxious. I choked back a gag, closing my hands over my mouth, fighting not to retch. I heard footsteps in the garage now, followed by muffled voices.

"The girls aren't in the basement."

"She got out."

"We'll catch them all on the road."

The garage door began grumbling open.

"They've taken the bicycles."

"We'll run them down. We'll have *all* of their blood."

I heard vehicle doors open and then close. *Thunk. Thunk.* An engine roared to life. I cracked the freezer door open and peeked out. Dumloch and Larch were sitting inside the van. The van moved, backing out of the garage.

The dynamite under the wheels!

No!

The image must have escaped my mind, because Ms. Larch picked up on it. I heard her velvety voice inside my head, a worried question: *What?*

Then the world exploded.

Twenty-two

I sensed that my head was filling with air, that it would continue filling until it finally burst. Pressure built behind my eyes. I had a horrible vision of them popping free from my skull. Then I was crashing through the darkness, my body banging from surface to surface. My knees, my elbows, my coccyx (butt), my head—slapping, cracking, and tumbling into oblivion.

Then nothing.

Forever.

Then the sounds of trickling, the blackness around me filling with water. My eyes were open, but I couldn't see! Were they open? Yes, I was blinking them! But then I grew tired of blinking them. I let them close. I listened to the falling water. And slept.

More nothing, only sleep, but not sleep—unconsciousness. I couldn't allow that. That was the kiss of death!

I had to fight. I couldn't let myself pass out. I had to stay awake. "Svetlana," I whispered into the darkness. *Svetlana* . . . I breathed my name and clung to the world.

Voices now.

"Over here!" someone shouted.

Splashing sounds, then thumping sounds as I was rocked in the blackness.

Suddenly, a stabbing light and cold water falling over my face. I squeezed my eyes against the brightness. Hands grabbed and pulled.

"I found someone!" the voice shouted.

I was lifted away.

Twenty-three

For the record, let me say that twenty-two sticks of dynamite are *way* too much. In fact, I shouldn't even be alive. The only reason I survived is that some of the dynamite failed to detonate. I guess that's one of the benefits of using unstable explosives, although I certainly don't recommend it.

I awoke in the hospital surrounded by those awful smells: alcohol and bleach and rubber and old feet. Why do hospitals have to smell like that, anyway? Would a nice, fragrant potpourri be so detrimental? I was up to my neck in crisp white sheets. The sterility tickled my nose. My eyes fluttered. Above, fluorescent lights glowed, swimming in the ceiling.

I breathed in deeply and found a smell I loved.

"Stephanie, baby," Mom whispered. Her face was next to my face, her cheeks damp with tears. Her lips pressed cool against my cheek. I didn't mind that she called me Stephanie—at least for the moment.

"Hey, sweetie," Dad said. He knelt at the other side of the bed, his hand on my hand.

"If I could," a voice interjected. A doctor stepped forward and leaned over the hospital bed. "Would you look straight ahead for me, Stephanie." He shined a bright penlight in my eyes, moving from one eye to the other before clicking it off and sliding it back into his jacket pocket. "Is this uncomfortable?" His hands moved across my forehead to the top of my head, probing.

"Ow," I winced.

Jerk.

"Can you wiggle your fingers and toes for me, Stephanie?"

The doctor observed as I frowned and wiggled. Dad's worried face peered over the doctor's shoulder.

"I'm fine, Dad," I croaked, squeezing one eye shut against the throbbing in my head. The ache was like a permanent ice-cream brain freeze.

"I don't think there's any call for concern, Mr. Grimm," the doctor said. He was scribbling on a clipboard. "Young people bounce so much better than we do, eh? A nasty knock on the head and probably a few bruises—nothing broken. I'd say we keep her in the hospital overnight for observation—just to be safe."

Mom's shiny eyes were close to my face again. "What in the world happened, Stephanie?"

"Ahem . . ." A tall man who'd been standing quiet and invisible against the wall stepped forward. He seemed almost to appear from thin air. "If I might ask a few questions, doctor? Mr. Grimm?" He had a long face and a prickly looking mustache. He was attempting to smile and not quite succeeding.

Dad was furious at the intrusion. Most people can't tell when my dad's angry—for one thing, he hardly ever is (he used to meditate). But there is something he does with his left eyebrow, just drops it a little lower than the right one and tugs it slightly toward his nose. When that happens—watch out! It was happening now as he turned to the tall man who I somehow already knew was a cop. He growled, "My daughter just woke up in the hospital, detective. Do you really think this is the best time to be asking your questions? Do you have a son or daughter? Would you think this an appropriate time if it was your family?"

Even Mom piped in, her mouth cutting a severe line across the bottom of her face. "I have to agree with my husband. We'll certainly help if we can, but I think any questions you have can wait until morning."

The cop nodded but continued anyway, his eyes moving from Mom to Dad to me. "I understand, folks—and agree with your concern—but I wouldn't be here if this wasn't urgent. The fact is we've got some banged-up, frightened kids on our hands, including three missing girls who've suddenly reappeared out of the blue. I've got a corpse in a car, a house blown to smithereens, and your daughter fished from the Flint River inside an icebox." His hard eyes measured me coolly before moving back to my parents. "I think we can all agree that I need to ask

Stephanie at least a few questions right now. There might be some dangerous people running around we need to know about."

Not anymore, I thought.

I reached up and gently pressed the knot at the top of my head. Pain pulsed dully, making me squint. Even in a fog, I knew I had to step carefully with this detective. I hadn't thought much beyond the confrontation with Ms. Larch—I hadn't thought beyond it at all, in fact. What kind of trouble could I be in here? Probably mountains of it.

The detective stepped to the edge of the bed and laid his hand firmly on my shoulder, eyeing my dad to make sure that was all right. He telegraphed a false smile, fixing me with gray eyes and a serious face. "Stephanie," he said, "what happened tonight?"

I'd definitely had enough of this "Stephanie" business. I slapped on a false expression of my own: bewilderment, with just a dash of confusion and sadness thrown in for good measure. I pressed the knot on my noggin and winced. "I don't remember a thing," I lied.

Twenty-four

After I returned home from the hospital, I found myself on serious restriction. I had to pull an extra-long face just to be let out in the yard. Razor and I were practically on the same leash. But Mom and Dad did allow me to deliver Ms. Bones her dinner in the evenings—even let me eat with her sometimes, just to keep her company. They thought Lenora Bones was simply the sweetest little old lady. Of course, they had no idea that I'd ridden ten pounds of that little old lady's dynamite into the Flint River.

"Knock, knock," I announced, tapping on the frosted glass of the back door. I elbowed the latch and stepped inside. Ms. Bones still had another week or so to go before she got out of her wheelchair.

Her voice grew from somewhere back in the house. "Is it dinnertime already? I declare—I'm like some potentate, being waited on hand and foot." She careened into the kitchen, banging into the table hard enough to topple the salt and pepper shakers. "Oh, dear." She steadied herself, pushing away from the table. "I haven't quite mastered this contraption."

I wondered if she'd been double-dipping into her painkillers. "You might want to let your leg mend before you go breaking it again."

Lenora Bones smiled. "I'll be back in tiptop condition in no time at all—thanks to your wonderful care. But how are *you* faring, my sweet?"

"Well, I haven't been arrested yet—if that's what you mean." I set down the foil-covered plates that were warming my hands.

Ms. Bones waved dismissively. "I wouldn't worry your head over that. *Criminals* can hardly get arrested nowadays—let alone angels such as yourself." She grabbed a handful of my cheek and squeezed. "Now let's eat!"

I uncovered the plates of ravioli.

"Good heavens," she said, "your mother *is* determined to put some meat on me."

I shrugged off my backpack and pulled up a chair. I dug into my pasta, already two bites behind. Despite appearances, the old lady could shovel away some serious food.

"I think you'll find worry a poor investment," she advised. "Your little team hasn't broken yet, have they?" Meaning Fumio and Foote. "Of course not. And if they haven't by now, believe me, they won't. Those boys don't want matters complicated any more than you do." She cocked an eyebrow. "I say let the authorities wrap things up as they please."

The dynamite explosion had left little of Larch's sports car and nothing at all of Dumloch's van—including Larch and Dumloch. Had the two been vaporized or atomized? Their vampire flesh obliterated and blown into dust? The Bone Lady believed so.

As far as the cops were concerned, Larch and Dumloch were prime suspects in what they assumed had been a botched kidnapping. They believed the teachers had been holding the three girls for ransom. The fact that Marsha and Madison's dad was some kind of millionaire helped sell that line of reasoning. The authorities theorized the dynamite explosion was a diversion set by the duo to aid in their escape. It sounded like brilliant detective work to me—more power to them. Foote, Fumio, and I had been dismissed as three clueless kids who just happened to pass along and spy the missing girls' bikes inside an open garage—accidental heroes foiling Larch and Dumloch's villainous scheme.

That worked—as long as Foote and Fumio didn't spill the beans about the dynamite.

"Don't fret," Ms. Bones said, sensing the worry still hounding my thoughts. "You've done excellent work, a terrific job: vanquished the dragon and saved the village and all that." She reached a hand to my elbow and squeezed. "You did what had to be done—and I'm very proud of you, Svetlana." She poked a forkful of pasta into her mouth, grinning. A dab of red sauce lingered on her lip, and she swiped with a napkin. "How's the cranium?"

"Good," I answered. After two weeks, the knot on my noggin had almost completely vanished.

"And your friend Dwight?"

"He's good," I said. "Getting better."

We finished, and I gathered up the plates.

"Be sure to give your mother my thanks, as usual. But no more—I can take care of myself, you know."

"I know, but just until you get back on your feet. Please?" *Please? At least until I'm off restriction?*

Very well, she thought, her words tickling like a feather behind my eyes. *But only because you're a dear and your mother's a wonderful cook.*

I reached beneath the chair and fished inside my backpack for *What Is Known.* I drew the book free and laid the heavy volume on the table. "I've finally finished," I said.

"And?"

"And it's scary stuff. Unbelievable."

"Very scary—and all true. But keep it a bit longer. Study it." She pushed the book back toward me. "And I've one other thing for you to take." She wheeled from the room and returned a moment later with a package across her lap. "It arrived for you in the mail today."

"For me?"

"Well, it has your name on it, my dear."

The box was wrapped in plain brown paper, stamped AIRMAIL, and peppered with postage bearing the likeness of the Queen of England. The address on the box was Lenora Bones's, but the addressee was SVETLANA GRIMM; the sender, BARTALBY FRIES AND FISH.

"Bartalby Fries and Fish?"

The old woman shrugged. "Sounds like a chip shop."

"What is it?" The package weighed as much as a phone book.

You can see I haven't opened it.

But you know, I thought.

"It's serious business, for certain—I can tell you that much. So be thoughtful when you unwrap it." She lifted a pop-knuckled finger to stay my hands. "But not now."

"Don't open it?" Then why was she giving it to me?

Because it's yours, Svetlana, if you like—or even if you don't like. As I've said before, we hardly have a choice. You're familiar with What Is Known, *so you know. You have a talent; that's a fact. What's in the box is like a promise. It's a promise that you make. If you truly accept.*

Accept? I lifted the box and shook it.

She said, "Tonight's close, but tomorrow night the moon will be full. Open it then—at midnight—outside if you can."

"But why then?"

Her thin lips curled at the ends. "To honor the moon, perhaps. It's a wonderful thing, after all—a light amidst all that darkness." She reached her fingers to my cheek, brushing gently. "So open it then. It's something of a tradition—or superstition. Something silly like that."

Twenty-five

"Can you believe this?" Fumio complained, taking a seat and sliding a paper across the lunchroom table to me.

I looked and saw it was an advance copy of the *Sunny Hill Bee*. I leafed through the four pages and didn't see anything special. A couple of articles welcoming the two new teachers, a piece on the success of this year's Spring Fling, a few puzzles and poems. "What?"

"That's right. 'What?' Mr. Horn didn't print one word of my story. He said it was inappropriate, that the school needed to move forward and put the past behind us." Mr. Horn was the newspaper editor.

"It was practically a made-up story, anyway," I said, tossing the paper back across the table to him.

Fumio scrunched up his face. "Factually inaccurate—slightly. But the spirit of the article was true." His account had thankfully not mentioned vampires, nor connected us directly to the dynamite—he was at least that smart. He knitted his brows. "And you said I'd end up getting a story out of this."

"Hey, there are always the tabloids," I suggested. "Give it a shot—mail something in. You might find yourself in every grocery store in the country."

"Maybe," Fumio said, but he shook his head doubtfully.

Foote approached, steadying his lunch tray with his one good arm.

"How's your bum wing, Dwight?" I asked.

He sat and shrugged. "It's better. Still a pain in the butt to get a decent night's sleep, though."

The short cast was gone from his left arm, but a full cast now enveloped his right arm, courtesy of his short flight on Dumloch Airlines. Luckily, the heavy drapes in the bedroom window and a prickly bush below had saved him from anything worse.

We'd both been pretty lucky. Just thinking about the explosion made me cringe. Lenora Bones thought I'd done a smashing job, but, really, I'd barely escaped being blown to smithereens.

For lunch I'd packed an apple and a double-decker sandwich: half tomato and half raspberry jam (I know, it sounds gross, but it's totally not). Before digging in, I reached over and sliced up Foote's cube steak without him even having to ask, which I guess was the least I could do.

"Thanks, Svet," he said with a smile, always pushing it. "You know, you haven't signed my new cast yet."

Why not? I found a blank spot amid the scribbles and added my two cents in black felt tip: "Always stay downstairs—Svetlana."

"Hardy-har," he said, blueberry eyes blinking.

"Hey, guys," Sandy said, joining us for lunch. She'd been sitting at our table all week. She's not so bad. Still with the lousy taste in clothes, but to each her own. What do I know about style, anyway?

"How much longer you got left on restriction, Svetlana?"

"Two more weeks to go," I told her. "My dad's easy, but Mom won't budge."

Sandy curled a finger in her mess of blond hair. "My folks are letting me put my trampoline back up. If you guys want, you could come over sometime."

Dwight perked up. "When my cast is off, sure—if my dad'll let me. He might not, though. He thinks I'm made of glass or something lately."

"Don't forget about your wooden head," Fumio added.

What a bunch of dodos. Dodo wannabes, actually. "Do any of you have a clue how many trampoline-related injuries occur in this country every year? Maybe we can do something else—a trip to the mall, even."

"Yeah," Sandy said, "but not to the mall. I don't care if I never see that place again."

Darwin would be proud.

When the bell rang for last period, I hustled to class. I couldn't afford to be late for science. After Larch's position opened up, Mom didn't have to substitute anymore—she became a full-time science teacher at Sunny Hill Middle School. She was low-key at home, but in class she acted like a general commanding troops. Attention! Still, she's definitely the best teacher ever.

But man, she loved to pile on the homework.

You think she'd cut me a break—I practically got her the job.

Twenty-six

The hands on the rooster neared midnight. I slid from beneath the bed and found the package in the closet. Moonlight fell in a long, pale block across the floor. I stood at the window, peering into the maze of shadows and light in the yard below. I hugged the package to my pajama top. Nothing moved on the streets beyond the fence. Windows in the nearby houses were as black as caves. A few porchlights glowed yellow and dull.

I silently descended the stairway, leaving Mom and Dad's soft breathing behind. Downstairs, wheels inside the grandfather clock clicked and whirred as the hands crept toward the hour. I turned at the ticking of Razor's nails across the hardwood floor.

"Good boy," I whispered, kneeling, scratching his neck. "Good boy, Razor." His eyes glistened in the dark, watching me. The fridge hummed. I moved toward the kitchen door. "Stay," I called softly over my shoulder, then stepped outside.

The moon was a bright hole poked in the sky, a cutout in the darkness. Light fell through, splashing the world in liquid silver, throwing everything into stark relief. The evening coolness seeped through my pajamas. I crossed the yard toward a wide pool of moonlight. My shadow fell around me in a black ring.

I knelt on the crisp grass and tore the wrapping from the package. I pushed my thumbnail along its taped center, splitting the folds of cardboard. Inside was a book. It was heavy; the cover, made of leather, was thick and soft. I thumbed through the empty pages. Squares of stark white reflected the lunar glow, waiting. Only a page near the front was marked—a symbol at its center: two circles each the size of a quarter, one white and one black, the natural and the aberrant, and where they met, a third circle, smaller, and red.

The red was dark in the moonlight, another version of black.

This is you.

Above, a flutter of wings and then gone. A night bird? A black carpet spread across the sky. Pale pinpricks for stars. The moon was a vast ivory eye, cold and distant. Inside the house, the grandfather clock began tolling midnight. I lifted my face toward the bathing light. I breathed deeply, filling myself, every sight and sound filtering through me.

I set the book aside and returned my attention to the package. I removed a slender case of dark wood and lifted its hinged top. Moonlight winked from a narrow blade, throwing light into my eyes. The blade was a duplicate of the one Ms. Bones carried in her boot, five inches of thin, polished steel. The instrument was cold; the handle, smooth and heavy.

Another twinkling came from within the case, a thread of silver. I lifted the necklace. A red stone dangled from the chain, obsidian in the moonlight. I pressed my thumb across the letters cut into the mounting, eight small grooves.

Svetlana

I turned the stone beneath the glowing heavens, reading the carved letters of my true name. I brought the clasp together behind my neck, making my promise, letting the silver lie cool against my skin, the stone at my sternum. Moonlight everywhere.

Thirteen days till I was off restriction.

I couldn't wait.

Lewis Harris has backpacked more than three thousand miles along the Appalachian Trail and hitchhiked to the Arctic Ocean. He's lived in the French Quarter of New Orleans, on a high mountain pass in Wyoming, and aboard a paddleboat on the Mississippi River. He's worked as a massage therapist, a short-order cook, a room-service waiter, and a janitor. But he's happiest being a writer. He now lives in Florida, and this is his first book. You can visit him online at **www.lewisharrisbooks.com.**

❧ Other books you may enjoy ❧

Deep and Dark and Dangerous

By Mary Downing Hahn

All the Lovely Bad Ones

By Mary Downing Hahn

Dillweed's Revenge

By Florence Parry Heide,
Illustrated by Carson Ellis

Sweet Miss Honeywell's Revenge

By Kathryn Reiss

**There's a Dead Person
Following My Sister Around**

By Vivian Vande Velde

**Tales from the Brothers Grimm
and the Sisters Weird**

By Vivian Vande Velde

43 Old Cemetery Road series

By Kate Klise • Illustrated by M. Sarah Klise

Dying to Meet You

Over My Dead Body

The Magic Shop Books

By Bruce Coville

Jeremy Thatcher,
Dragon Hatcher

Jennifer Murdley's Toad

The Monster's Ring

The Skull of Truth

Juliet Dove, Queen of Love

Secrets of Dripping Fang series

By Dan Greenburg • Illustrated by Scott M. Fischer

The Onts

Treachery and
Betrayal at Jolly Days

The Vampire's Curse

Fall of the House
of Mandible

The Shluffmuffin
Boy Is History

Attack of the
Giant Octopus

Please Don't Eat
the Children

When Bad Snakes
Attack Good Children

www.hmhbooks.com